Cara chanced a look ahead, watching Nicholas from behind.

Nicholas glanced sideways at the fields they rode beside, a smile curving his lips.

This is where he belongs, Cara thought, looking at him now silhouetted against the mountains. This is his natural setting.

Pain twisted Cara's heart.

And where do you belong?

Before she met Nicholas the question had resonated through her life. Then, for those few, magical months with Nicholas, she'd thought she had found her place.

And now?

She was expending too much energy wondering how to react to Nicholas and thinking of how to behave around him.

They were outside on this beautiful day and were headed out into the hills. *Just enjoy it. Don't put extra burdens on it.*

Nicholas sat easily on his horse, his one hand on his thigh, the other loosely holding the reins. He had rolled his shirtsleeves over his forearms, and as he rode, she could see his broad shoulders moving ever so slightly in response to the movement of the horse.

He's an extremely good-looking man, she thought with a touch of wistfulness.

And he doesn't belong to you anymore.

Books by Carolyne Aarsen

Love Inspired

CAROLYNE AARSEN

and her husband, Richard, live on a small ranch in northern Alberta, where they have raised four children and numerous foster children and are still raising cattle. Carolyne crafts her stories in her office with a large west-facing window through which she can watch the changing seasons while struggling to make her words obey.

Cattleman's Courtship
Carolyne Aarsen

Steeple
Hill®

Published by Steeple Hill Books™

STEEPLE HILL BOOKS

Steeple
Hill®

Recycling programs
for this product may
not exist in your area.

ISBN-13: 978-0-373-81488-6

CATTLEMAN'S COURTSHIP

Copyright © 2010 by Carolyne Aarsen

www.SteepleHill.com

Printed in U.S.A.

I have learned to be content whatever
the circumstances.
—*Philippians* 4:11

I'd like to dedicate this book to Linda Ford, my friend and critique partner. You rejoice with me and weep with me and help me struggle with stories. Especially this one. You are an inspiration and an encouragement. I couldn't do what I do without your help.

Chapter One

Panic spiraled through Cara Morrison as she stared at the cowboy standing with his back to her looking at a chart on the wall of the vet clinic.

Nicholas Chapman. The man she was once engaged to. The man she thought she didn't care for anymore.

He wasn't supposed to be back in Alberta, Canada. He was supposed to be working overseas.

And she wasn't supposed to be reacting to her ex-fiancé this way.

The familiar posture, the slant of his head with its broad cowboy hat, the breadth of his shoulders, his one hand slung up in the front pocket of his faded blue jeans all pulled at old memories Cara thought she had pushed aside.

Bill, the other vet, was out on call and her uncle had chosen this exact time to grab a cup of coffee, leaving the clinic in her capable hands, he had said. If she'd known who the next client would be, she wouldn't have let him leave!

Nicholas turned and Cara's heart slowed for a few heavy beats, then started up again. She sucked in a quick breath as her mouth went dry.

Gray eyes, the color of a summer storm, met hers in a piercing gaze. Eyes she had once looked into with love and caring. Eyes that once beheld her with warmth instead of the coolness she now observed.

"Hello, Cara. I heard rumors you were back in town." Nicholas pushed his hat back on his head, his well-modulated voice showing no hint of discomfort.

The last time she saw him, three years ago, he wasn't as in control. His anger had spilled over into harsh words that cut and hurt. And instead of confronting him, challenging him, she had turned tail and run.

And she and Nicholas hadn't spoken since then.

Her friend Trista had assured her Nicholas was working overseas on yet another dangerous job.

Yet here he stood making her heart pound and her face flush.

"I'm visiting my aunt and uncle for a week," she said, forcing a smile to her face, thankful the trembling in her chest didn't translate to her voice. "After that I'm heading to Europe for a holiday."

"What made you decide Europe?"

Okay, chitchat. She could do chitchat.

"My mother spent some time in Malta."

"Ah, yes. In her many travels around the world."

Cara frowned at the faint tone of derision in his voice. Though Cara had wished and prayed that her mother would stay with her instead of heading off on yet another mission project, she also had wished she shared her mother's zeal.

"She did some relief work there," Cara said. "I'd like to visit the orphanage where she worked." She folded her arms over her chest. "And how are things with you and your father?"

"We're busy on the ranch," he replied. He drew his hands out of the pockets of his denim jeans and placed them on the counter.

The hands of a working man. Cara fleetingly noticed the faint scars on the backs of his hands, a black mark on one fingernail.

His eyes bored into hers and for the smallest moment she felt like taking a step back at the antagonism she saw there. But she clung to the counter, holding her ground.

"And how are you enjoying Vancouver?" he asked.

"I'm moving."

Nicholas raised one eyebrow. "Where to this time?"

"I've got a line on a job in Montreal working for an animal drug company in a lab."

He gave a short laugh. "Didn't figure you for a big-city person working in a lab."

"The job is challenging." She gave a light shrug, as if brushing away his observations.

At one time this man held her heart in the callused hands resting on the counter between them. At one time all her unspoken dreams and wishes for a family and a place were pinned on this man.

She couldn't act as if he were simply another customer she had to deal with. "What can I do for you?" she asked, going directly to the point.

He gave her a smile that held no warmth and in spite of her own hurt it still cut.

"I need to vaccinate my calves before I put them out to pasture."

"How many doses?" she asked, sliding the large glass refrierator door open and pulling out the boxes he asked for.

"Anything else?" she asked, favoring him with a quick glance, hoping she looked far more professional than she felt.

"Yeah. I'm sending a shipment of heifers to

the United States. I need to know what I have to do before I send them out."

"From your purebred herd?"

Nicholas nodded, reaching up to scratch his forehead with one finger. He often did that when he contemplated something, Cara thought. She was far too conscious of his height, of the familiar lines of his face. The way his hair always wanted to fall over his forehead. How his dark eyebrows accented the unusual color of his eyes. How his cheekbones swept down to his firm chin.

He looks tired.

The thought slipped past her defenses, awakening old feelings she thought she had dealt with.

She crossed her arms as if defending herself against his heartrending appeal.

"I'm sending out my first shipment of heifers along with a bull," he continued. "If this guy likes what he sees, I could have a pretty good steady market."

"You're ranching full-time now?" Cara fought the strong urge to step back, to give herself more space away from the easy charm that was causing her tension.

Nicholas frowned, shaking his head. "After I ship out the heifers I'm heading overseas again."

"Overseas?" She'd been told that, but she didn't know the details. Guess working offshore rigs wasn't dangerous enough, or didn't pay enough. "Where will you be?"

"A two-month stint in Kuwait. Dad's still able to take care of the ranch so I figure I better work while I can."

"And how's your leg?" she asked, referring to the accident he suffered working on the rigs just before their big fight. The fight that had shown Cara that Nicholas's ranch would always come before anything or anyone else in his life. Including her.

Nicholas eyes narrowed. "The leg is fine."

"Glad to hear it."

Before they could get into another dead-end discussion, Cara pulled a pad of paper toward her. "As for the heifers you'll be shipping, you'll need to call the clinic to book some tests." Was that her voice? So clipped, so tense? She thought after three years she would be more relaxed, more in control.

She reached for a pen but instead spilled the can's contents all over the counter with a hollow clatter.

Of course, she thought, grabbing for the assortment of pens. Nicholas Chapman shows up and hands that could stitch up a tear in a kitten's eyelid without any sign of a tremor suddenly become clumsy and awkward.

"Here, let me help you," he said as he picked up the can and set it upright.

For the briefest of moments, their hands brushed each other. Cara jerked hers back.

Nicholas dropped the handful of pens into the aluminum can, then stood back.

Cara didn't look at him as she scribbled some instructions and put them in her uncle's appointment book. "I made a note for my uncle to call you, in case you or your dad forget." She didn't want to sound so aloof, but how else could she get through this moment?

He took the paper she handed him and, after glancing down briefly at it, folded it up and slipped it into his pocket. "I could have phoned for the information, but I was in town anyway."

He'd heard she was around, but was seeing her as much of a shock to him as to her?

He grabbed the bag, murmured his thanks then left. As the door swung shut behind him, relief sluiced through her.

Their first meeting had finally happened.

Maybe now she could finally get past her old feelings for him and get on with her life.

It had been three years since they'd broken up over the very thing they had talked about. His blind devotion to his ranch and his commitment to working dangerous jobs that paid high wages, which all went back into the ranch.

When she found out he'd broken his leg on one of his jobs, she'd been sick with worry. After his accident, she'd pleaded with Nicholas to quit working the rigs. But he hadn't even entertained the idea.

When he'd left, when he chose the work over her, she'd left, too.

She'd come back to Cochrane periodically, but only when she was sure he was gone. So they had never talked about her sudden departure and they had never met each other face-to-face. Until now.

Cara wished she could do exactly what Trista, her best friend, had been telling her ever since she left. Get over Nicholas. Start dating.

Trouble was she had no interest in dating. She never did.

As a young girl, she had moved every couple of years as her mother sought the elusive perfect job. Each move meant pulling up roots and breaking ties.

Then, at age fifteen, she moved in with her aunt and uncle in Cochrane. Determined to make something of herself, she applied herself to her studies and worked summers in her uncle's vet clinic.

It wasn't until she graduated medical school and started working at her uncle's clinic full-time that she met Nicholas and truly fell in love for the first time. They dated for six months and got engaged.

And six months later they broke up.

Though she knew she had to get over him, seeing him just now was much, much harder than she'd thought it would be.

One thing was sure, Cara couldn't stay, knowing she'd run into Nicholas again. Her reaction to him showed her that quite clearly.

She'd stay the weekend and go to church with her aunt and uncle. Then, on Monday she would be on the phone to a travel agent getting her ticket changed as soon as possible.

Nicholas adjusted his corduroy blazer, straightened the tie cinching his collared shirt and shook his head at his own preening.

Since when, he asked himself, *did you get so fussed about what you look like when you go to church?*

Since he knew Cara Morrison would be attending. He had almost changed his mind about going this morning. He had to trim horses' hooves and check fences, but at the same time he felt a strong need to be at church. When he worked rigs, he couldn't attend at all, so he when he had a chance to worship with fellow believers, he took it.

He turned away from his image in the bathroom mirror and jogged down the stairs.

His father was rooting through the refrigerator and looked up when Nicholas entered the kitchen.

Dale Chapman still wore his cowboy hat and boots. Obviously he'd been out checking the cows already this morning. He was a tall, imposing man and, in his youth, had been trim and fit.

Now his stomach protruded over the large belt buckle, a remnant from his rodeo years that had taken his time and money and given him a bum back and a permanent limp. Though his hair was gray, he still wore it long in the back.

"What's with all this vaccine?" He pulled out one of the boxes Nicholas had purchased yesterday.

"I thought we were out."

Dale Chapman narrowed his eyes. "I heard that Morrison girl was back in town," his father said as Nicholas pulled out the coffeepot and found it empty. "Is that the reason you went to the vet clinic?"

Nicholas shrugged off the question, wishing away a sudden flush of self-consciousness as he pulled the boiling kettle off the stove and rinsed off an apple. Not the most balanced breakfast, but it would hold him until lunchtime.

"If you think she's going to change her mind you're crazy," Dale said as he pulled a carton of milk out of the fridge. "She's not a rancher's wife and we all know how that can turn out."

Nicholas ignored his father's little speech as he poured grounds and hot water into the coffee press. Though it had been fifteen years since Nicholas's parents' divorce, Dale had mistrusted women ever since. And that mistrust had seeped into his opinion of Cara. His father's negative opinion of Cara Morrison hadn't been encouraging when he and Cara were dating. When Cara broke off the engagement, Dale had tried and failed not to say "I told you so" in many ways, shapes and forms.

"How long she around for this time?" his father asked, pouring the milk over his bowl of cereal.

"Didn't ask."

"Probably not long, if she's like her mom."

Nicholas didn't say anything, knowing nothing was required, and he wasn't going to get pulled into a conversation about Cara.

He thought he had been prepared to see her again. Thought he had successfully pushed her out of his mind. Hadn't he even dated a number of other girls since Cara?

Again he could feel the miscreant beat of his heart when he turned and saw her standing behind the counter, almost exactly as she had the first time they had met.

That first time he'd seen her, he'd been enchanted with her wide eyes, an unusual shade of brown. The delicate line of her face. She had looked so fragile.

But he knew better.

He'd seen her covered in mud, rain streaming down her face as she helped deliver a foal. He'd seen her do a Cesarean section on a cow in the freezing cold, seen her manhandle calves that weighed almost as much as she did.

Cara Morrison was anything but fragile.

And he was anything but over her.

She left without a word, he told himself. *She couldn't even break up with you to your face. She ran away instead of facing things. Get over it.*

So why was he going to church knowing he might see her?

Because he wasn't the kind of person to run away or get chased away.

He had some pride, he thought, finishing off his apple and tossing the core into the garbage can. And because, when he stayed away from church, his heart felt empty and his soul unnourished.

He said a quick goodbye to his father and ran to his truck. He was already running late.

Half an hour later a helpful usher escorted him to one of the few empty spots in the building. He sat down, got settled in and ended up looking directly at the back of Cara Morrison's head.

He glanced around, looking for another place to sit, but then the minister came to the front of the church and encouraged everyone to rise and greet their neighbors.

Nicholas immediately turned to the person beside him and then Cara's aunt called out his name. Was it his imagination or did Cara jump?

"So good to see you here," Lori Morrison said, catching his hand. He shook Lori's hand and then, with a sense of inevitability, turned to Cara.

She gave him a tight smile but didn't offer to shake his hand. "Good morning, Nicholas. Good to see you again."

"Is it?"

The words came out before he could stop them.

Well, that was brilliant. Nicholas watched Cara slowly turn away from him. Why couldn't he be as cool as she was? Why couldn't he return her greeting instead of running the risk of antagonizing her again?

Now she stood with her back to him, the overhead lights catching glints of gold in her hair. Three years ago she wore it short, like a cap. Now it brushed her shoulders, inviting touch.

He crossed his arms, angry at his reaction to her. It had been three years. It was done.

And Nicholas spent the rest of the church

service alternately trying to listen to the minister and trying to ignore Cara Morrison.

He was successful at neither.

Finally the minister spoke the benediction. The congregation rose for the final song. As soon as the last note rang out and the minister stood at the back of the church, Nicholas made his escape.

He had his hand on the bar that opened the exterior door when he heard someone call his name. His first impulse was to ignore whoever called him. And he would have managed if the helpful person behind him hadn't tapped him on the shoulder.

"I believe Mrs. Hughes wants to talk to you," his neighbor said. He pointed out a thin, short woman waving at him from the top of the stairs in the foyer.

Nicholas smiled his acknowledgment and, with a sigh of resignation, walked back through the crowd of people in the foyer.

He had his hand on the handrail of the steps and looked up in time to see Cara walking down the stairs past Mrs. Hughes.

Cara caught his eye, then glanced quickly away.

Right behind her stood her uncle, Alan Morrison.

Nicholas caught Alan's piercing gaze. It was as if he were making sure Nicholas didn't "hurt" his precious niece yet again. Nicholas wanted to reassure him that as far as Cara was concerned, he had gotten the memo long ago.

Then Nicholas saw a look of puzzlement cross Alan's face as his step faltered. Alan's hand clutched the handrail on his right side as he cried out.

Then, as if in slow motion, he crumpled and folded in on himself.

Cara turned. Her aunt Lori screamed.

And as Nicholas watched in horror, Alan Morrison fell heavily down the rest of the stairs.

Nicholas was the first one at his side. Cara right behind him. "Call an ambulance," Nicholas shouted to the people who now milled around.

"Stretch him out." Cara pulled on Alan's arm, falling to her knees beside him. "Straighten him out and open his coat."

Alan's face held a sickly gray tinge, his eyes like dark bruises, unfocused, staring straight up.

As Nicholas unbuttoned Alan's suit jacket, Cara placed her hand above his mouth then, bending over, put her mouth on his and gave him two quick breaths.

Her fingers swept his neck, pressing against it.

"No pulse," she murmured.

"I'll do the CPR, you take care of the breathing."

Nicholas counted to himself, one and two, pressing down on each count. Cara was bent over her uncle's head, breathing for him.

Nicholas felt vaguely aware of the people around them as they worked, Lori crying, someone else telling people to move away.

But for Nicholas, the only thing that existed was the two of them fighting to save Cara's beloved uncle's life. A tiny cosmos among the shifting crowd around them.

He didn't know how long they worked. It seemed like a few moments, a brief snatch of time.

Yet by the time someone called out to make room for the paramedics, the tension knotted his shoulders and the hard floor dug into his knees.

"I'll take over, sir." Hands pulled him back as others caught the rhythm he had maintained.

Nicholas caught the glimpse of two uniformed men and he got slowly to his feet, his legs tingling as the blood rushed back to them.

Another paramedic strapped an oxygen mask on Alan's head, manually pumping life-giving oxygen into him.

Cara sat back, her hands hanging slack by her side, her eyes huge in her pale face.

Nicholas tried to work his way around Alan to be at her side. But someone else took her by the shoulders. Lifted her up. Held her as she visibly trembled.

That's my job, my place, he thought, feeling ineffective and surprisingly possessive as someone else stroked her hair in comfort.

In a flurry of activity the paramedics had Alan on a stretcher and then wheeled him out the doors.

Beyond the double doors Nicholas saw the whirling lights atop the ambulance and the enormity of what had just happened struck him.

"Cara. Go with him," Nicholas heard Lori Morrison called out.

Cara glanced around, looking confused at the sound of her aunt's voice.

"Please," Lori pleaded. "I can't. I just can't."

Nicholas found her this time and gave her a gentle push in the direction of the ambulance. "I'll take care of your aunt. You go. Be with your uncle."

He gave her shoulder a quick squeeze before she whirled away, running after the paramedics.

Nicholas hurried to Lori's side. "I'll take you to the hospital," he said, slipping his arm over her shoulder. "We'll meet Cara there."

Lori only nodded, clutching his arm.

He steered Lori to his truck and soon they were

speeding down the highway to the hospital, trying in vain to keep up with the ambulance. Lori sat curled against the passenger's-side window, a silent figure clutching her coat, her face strobed by the flashing red lights of the ambulance they were following.

While he drove, Nicholas sent up a quick prayer for Alan Morrison and for Cara, praying the ambulance would get to the hospital on time.

Chapter Two

Sorrow, huge as a stone, lodged in Cara's chest. Tears threatened, but she held them back. In the past couple of hours her aunt had cried enough for both of them.

She wanted time to rewind. She wanted to go back when her uncle was still walking around. Still talking and telling his terrible jokes.

Not strapped to a gurney with a paramedic working on him while they raced to the hospital in the swaying ambulance.

Myocardial infarction, the paramedics had said. Heart attack.

How could a heart suddenly decide to stop working? What triggered it?

Images flickered in her mind. Uncle Alan wheezing as he lifted a box. His unusually high color.

Though he only worked part-time, Cara knew

he'd been under stress lately. The practice had been extremely busy and Alan was called more often to fill in on the large animal work.

Another vet, Gordon Moen, was supposed to be coming to help out, but he wasn't arriving for another three weeks.

Too late for Uncle Alan.

The stone in her chest shifted and tears thickened her throat.

Please, Lord, don't take him away, too. You already took my mother, please spare him.

Then she caught herself.

God didn't listen to prayers. How many had she sent up that her mother would come back to her? Would put her first in her life?

Had God listened when she prayed Nicholas would choose her over his work? Over his ranch?

Sometimes she wondered if her prayers were selfish but she believed that anyone else in her situation would want the same things.

Aunt Lori always said God moved in mysterious ways. Well, they were certainly mysterious to Cara.

Cara rolled her head slightly, chancing a glance at Nicholas, who had stayed at the hospital. The knot of his tie hung below his open collar of his rumpled shirt. She couldn't help the hitch of her heart at the sight. He looked more approachable now, more like the Nicholas she remembered.

As if aware of her scrutiny, he glanced back at her. And again their gazes locked. He turned, then walked back in her direction.

He sat down in the empty chair beside her, resting his elbows on his knees. "How are you doing?" he asked.

The deep timbre of his voice still made her heart sing. Still swept away her natural reserve.

"I'm okay."

He frowned, as if dissatisfied with her reply. But what else could she say? She felt especially vulnerable now and if she said more, she would start to cry. She needed to maintain what dignity she could. To stay aloof, calm and in control. Nothing had changed in his life and she couldn't put herself through that emotional wringer once again.

"Here's your aunt," he said suddenly, standing up.

Lori came down the hallway, clutching her purse. A nurse walked beside her, talking in hushed tones. As they came closer Cara heard snatches of the conversation.

"He'll be on the monitors for a couple of days… good pulse…healthy man…"

Lori nodded, but Cara knew she wasn't absorbing all this.

Cara got up, stretching her tired muscles, and walked toward her aunt.

"How is he?" Cara knew the question was superfluous but she had to ask.

Her aunt shook her head. "He looks so awful with all those things attached to him. You don't want to see him yet."

But Cara needed to.

"Can I see him?" she asked the nurse.

"You two can go in," she said, gesturing at Cara. "But only for a minute. We don't want to tire him out."

Cara realized with a start the nurse had included Nicholas in the invitation. She was about to correct her, when the nurse turned, her shoes squeaking on the gleaming floor.

Cara didn't look back to see if Nicholas was coming, but as she followed the nurse, she could hear his measured tread behind her, slightly slower than her own.

The nurse motioned for Cara to come closer. "You've got two minutes then I'll come and get you." She smiled at Cara, then past her. Cara could tell the moment her smile connected with Nicholas. Nicholas always had that effect on women, she thought dully, pushing aside the curtain around her uncle's bed, her fingers trembling.

She stepped forward, then faltered at the sight before her.

Her uncle, a large, strapping man, lay on the bed, his face still obscured by the oxygen mask. Lines attached to circular pads snaked out to a machine beeping out a regular rhythm. His arms lay beside him, bare except for a blood-pressure cuff attached to a machine. Two IVs ran out from his arms.

He looked like death.

Cara pressed her hand to her mouth, stopping the faint cry of dismay, her knees buckling beneath her.

She would have fallen, but strong arms caught her from behind. Held her. Just for those few seconds she allowed herself to drift back against Nicholas's comforting strength, thankful for his presence.

We fit so well, Cara thought, letting him support her. His touch, his smell, his warmth felt so familiar it created an ache deep in her chest.

Then, when she caught her balance, his hands settled on her waist, held a moment and then gently pushed her away.

As if he couldn't stand to touch her any longer than he had to.

Cara disguised the pain of his withdrawal by catching her uncle's hand and clinging it to it, hoping he would pull through this emergency.

She stayed by her uncle's side a moment longer, then turned away.

"I want to…go," she said to Nicholas.

Aunt Lori sat huddled in the hard plastic chair, her hands kneading each other. As Cara came closer, her head came up. "Is he awake?"

Cara shook her head.

"He was working too hard." Aunt Lori's voice sounded so small. So wounded.

Cara stifled the flicker of guilt her aunt's innocent comment created. It wasn't her fault, she reminded herself. Even if she had stayed behind and worked at the clinic as her uncle had always envisioned, Alan Morrison wouldn't have slowed down. Wouldn't have done less.

"We should go home," Cara said quietly, taking her aunt's arm in hers.

"Can we come back tonight?"

"Of course we can. But you should go home and rest a bit before we do." Cara took her aunt's arm and, as they walked to the door, she leaned heavily on Cara.

The air outside smelled fresh, new. The sun shone down with a benevolent spring warmth, but Cara couldn't stop the chill shivering down her spine.

"My truck is parked over here," Nicholas said, stepping ahead of them to lead the way.

Cara acknowledged his comment with a

nod, following him more slowly, holding her aunt up.

"I made him eat his vegetables. I made him go for walks," Aunt Lori was saying, clutching Cara's arm. "I took good care of him."

"Of course you did," Cara said quietly, her attention split between her aunt and the man who strode in front of them, leading the way to his truck.

He opened the door and Cara felt a jolt of dismay. The cab had one bench seat with a fold-down console.

Which meant her aunt would be sitting by the window and Cara…right beside Nicholas.

She helped her aunt into the truck, then had to walk around to Nicholas's side. She began to get in slowly, wishing she'd worn sensible shoes instead of high heels made for walking short distances, not climbing running boards of pickup trucks.

She faltered as she stepped up and Nicholas caught her, his hand on her elbow. She tried to ignore his touch, wished her heart didn't jump at his nearness.

She settled on the seat beside her aunt, and buckled herself in. Nicholas got in and Cara's senses heightened.

"Can you move over a bit," Aunt Lori asked,

nudging Cara with her elbow. "I'm feeling claustrophobic."

Cara shifted as much as she dared. No matter what, though, she sat too close to Nicholas. She felt the warmth of his arm through the sleeve of her sweater and the scent of his cologne drew up older memories of other trips in this truck. Trips when she didn't mind sitting as close to him as she was now and often tried to sit even closer.

That's over, she thought.

The trip back to Cochrane was quiet, broken only by the hum of the tires on the pavement, the intermittent noise of the fan sending cooling air over the truck's occupants.

Cara kept her arms folded over her purse and tried, like her aunt did, to keep her eyes fixed on the road rolling past them.

But she couldn't stop her awareness of the man sitting next to her. Each curve in the road and each bump in the pavement brought the two of them in contact with each other.

"Did the doctor say anything about what might have caused the heart attack?" Nicholas asked, breaking the heavy silence.

Cara took a breath. "He told me his cholesterol levels were high. And I imagine the stress of working added to that."

"Did they say how serious it was?"

"A heart attack is serious. Period," Aunt Lori

said in a tone that didn't encourage any further discussion.

A heavy silence followed her remark. Cara wished she dared turn the radio on. She wished she and her aunt could share casual conversation. Anything to keep the picture of her uncle falling down the stairs out of her mind.

Anything to keep her from being so sensitive to Nicholas's presence.

The beginnings of a headache pinched her temples and by the time Nicholas pulled up to her aunt and uncle's home, Cara felt as if a vise gripped her forehead.

"Thanks for all your help," Aunt Lori said, leaning past Cara to give Nicholas a worn smile. Then she stepped out of the truck and headed up the walk to the house.

Cara slid over and from a safer distance risked a glance at Nicholas.

He draped one arm over the steering wheel, his other across the back of the seat, bringing his fingertips inches from her shoulder.

"Thanks for the ride and for all the help," Cara said. "I'm so glad you could bring Aunt Lori to the hospital."

Nicholas didn't say anything, his eyes holding hers. "Are you going to be okay?" His voice sounded cool, as if he were asking a mere acquaintance.

Cara shrugged and slipped her purse over her arm. "I don't know."

Quiet fell again and Cara didn't have anything more to say. So she slipped out of the truck and trudged up the sidewalk. But before she got to the house, she couldn't help a glance back over her shoulder.

Nicholas was watching her.

She took a chance and lifted her hand in a small wave, but he started his truck and drove away.

Cara closed her hand and pressed it to her chest, surprised at the jab of hurt.

Did you expect him to come running down the walk, pull you into his arms and beg you to give you another chance? Did you really think he was pining for you the whole time you were gone? He doesn't care for you anymore.

The words mocked her, and she turned and entered the house.

Aunt Lori sat in her usual chair in the kitchen, her arms wrapped around her midsection.

"Do you want some tea?" Cara asked, walking to the stove.

Aunt Lori nodded.

While she waited for the water to boil, Cara joined her aunt, glancing around the papers piled up on the room table, the dishes scattered over the kitchen counter. She wished she had the energy to start cleaning.

Her aunt was not a housekeeper. She always joked that she preferred to paint walls than wash them and she could always afford to get someone to do it for her.

Though she missed her aunt and uncle, she didn't miss the mess either in the house or her uncle's vet clinic. Her mother wasn't much different and at times Cara wondered if she really was a Morrison. Every time she came back to her aunt and uncle's place, either from university or visiting, she spent the first few days tidying up.

However, in spite of the chaos, Uncle Alan and Aunt Lori's home had been Cara's most stable home since Audra Morrison dropped Cara off at their place. Audra had assumed Cara was old enough to be without her while she followed her conscience and went to work overseas.

Cara still remembered the grim voice of her uncle, trying to plead with his sister, Cara's mother, to think of Cara.

Her mother's reply still rang in her ears. Cara had been raised with more privileges than any of the children she left to help. She didn't need her mother as much as these destitute young orphans in Nicaragua.

And then she left. Aunt Lori had come upstairs and had sat beside Cara, not saying anything, simply holding her close, letting Cara's tears drench the front of her shirt.

When Cara turned fifteen, everything changed. Cara's mother was killed flying into the Congo to help yet another group of lost and broken children.

And Cara was alone.

Uncle Alan and Aunt Lori were named her guardians. They paid for all her expenses, bought her a car. Put her through vet school and Uncle Alan offered her a job when she was done.

She started working for her uncle, met Nicholas and she thought her life had finally come to the place she'd been yearning for since she was a young girl.

A home of her own. A family of her own.

And now, her uncle lay in a hospital bed and Nicholas was more removed from her than ever.

"How are you doing?" Cara asked, reaching over and covering her aunt's icy hands with hers.

"I'm tired. And I'm scared." Lori looked up at Cara. "Will you pray with me?"

Cara was taken momentarily aback. How could her aunt talk about praying after what had just happened? What good would it do?

But she wasn't about to take what little comfort her aunt might derive from praying, away from her.

"Sure. I'll pray with you." Cara folded her hands over her aunt's and bowed her head.

Cara waited, then realized her aunt wanted her to do the praying.

Her heart fluttered in panic. What was she going to say? But her aunt squeezed her hands, signaling her need. So Cara cleared her throat and began.

"Dear Lord, Thank You for today…" She paused there, wondering what she could be thankful about when her uncle was so ill, but she carried on. "Thank You that we could worship with Your people in Your house…" She stopped, hearing the inauthentic words in her own ears.

She glanced up in time to see Aunt Lori looking over at her.

"Why did you stop, honey?"

Cara sighed. "I sound like Uncle Alan."

"That's not so bad."

Cara gave her aunt a quick smile. "No, but…"

"It's not from your heart." Aunt Lori finished the sentence for her.

"I don't know if I can pray from my heart." Cara tightened her grip on her aunt's hands.

"Why not?" Aunt Lori asked, her smile sad.

Cara sighed lightly, knowing she would have to

be honest with her aunt. "I don't think I've been able to pray since…"

"Audra died?" Aunt Lori stroked Cara's hand with her thumbs.

"Mom's death was the beginning."

"And what was the end?"

Cara looked down, working her lower lip between her teeth. "I know it sounds kind of funny now, maybe even a bit childish, but after Nicholas and I broke up, I haven't been able to pray at all."

"That was a hard time for you."

"Not as hard as what you're dealing with right now."

"I still have Alan's love. I know how much you cared for Nicholas and I know the hurt he caused in your life made you pull further away from God." Aunt Lori looked down at their joined hands, her thumbs still making their soothing circles around Cara's hand. "I hoped that by asking you to pray, you would be able to at least let God's love fill you. Let God break down that barrier you've put up between you and Him."

"He was the one that put it up, Aunt Lori," Cara whispered.

"God always seeks us," Aunt Lori assured her. "He never puts up walls. We do."

Cara's soul twisted and turned. "Love hurts, Aunt Lori. It hurts so much."

Her aunt reached out and cupped her cheek. "That's the risk of loving, my dear girl."

Cara let the words settle into the wrenching of her soul. She knew her aunt was right, but she also knew, for now, she wasn't going to take the chance of getting hurt again.

"I'll pray this time," Aunt Lori said, taking her hands.

Cara bowed her head and let her aunt's prayer wash over her. And for the merest moment, she felt a nudging against the walls she'd put around her heart.

She knew that everything had changed. In the space of a heartbeat, or lack of a heartbeat, her world had spun around.

There was no way she could wander around the streets of Malta knowing that her uncle, the man she thought of as her father, lay helpless and recuperating from a devastating heart attack.

She had no choice now. She would have to cancel her trip and stay in Cochrane to support her aunt. Even if it meant running the risk of seeing Nicholas and having her pain reinforced.

Though she had told her aunt she didn't pray much, she caught herself praying that when the time came she would be able to leave with her heart still intact.

Nicholas pulled up to his father's house and slammed on the brakes, dust swirling around his

truck as it fishtailed then abruptly stopped. He
was being juvenile and he knew it, but his anger
and frustration had to find some release and driving like a fool seemed to be a part of it.

The events of the past days piled on top of
each other. Seeing Cara in at the clinic then at
church. She acted so cool. So remote. He knew
part of it was his own fault. He'd put up his own
barriers to her and he had to remind himself to
keep them up.

Like you did at the hospital?

For a brief moment, when he and Cara had
seen Alan lying on the hospital bed, he thought
she might lean on him just a little longer. But
she had quickly pulled herself together and had
drawn away from his support.

Nicholas grabbed his tie from the seat and
opened the door, his anger fading with each
moment. He felt tired and drained. In the next
couple of weeks he had to get fences fixed, his
haying done and then get ready for another work
trip overseas.

He sighed as he trudged up the sidewalk. He
wished he could stay home, at the ranch. Wished
he could get on his horse and head up into the
mountains.

He thought of Cara's past insistence that he not
go back to work and the ensuing fight that had
sent her running.

Nicholas stopped at the top step of the house and, turning, let his eyes drift over the valley spread out before him. Cattle dotted the pasture near the house. His purebred herd painstakingly built up by him and his father over the past five years, had been paid for by the work he did.

Beyond this valley lay the land he and his father had purchased back from the bank after his parents' divorce. When missed payments led to foreclosure, this, too, had been paid for by his work. He had focused his entire life on this ranch.

He could have found work closer by, but it wouldn't have paid near what he got from working on oil rigs. The time off gave him the opportunity to work on the ranch. His father managed the ranch while he was gone. All in all it had been a convenient and lucrative arrangement.

One he wasn't in a position to change. Not yet. He knew the beating his father's pride took when they had to go, hat in hand, to the bank to refinance the ranch.

Four generations of Chapmans had farmed and ranched on this land and each generation had added to it and expanded it. Nicholas was the fifth generation and he wasn't going to let the ranch fail on his watch.

He knew Cara couldn't understand. She didn't have his attachment to the land. She didn't have the continuity of family and community he had. Though he didn't appreciate his father's puzzling antagonism toward Cara, he did agree with his father on one point.

Cara's lack of strong roots made it hard for her to appreciate the generations of sweat equity poured into this place. She couldn't understand how important the ranch was to him and to his father.

And if she didn't get that, then she wasn't the girl for him. Logically he knew his father was right about that.

He just had to convince his heart.

Chapter Three

"And how's Uncle Alan?" Cara asked, shifting the phone to her other hand as she slowed the car down and steered it around a tight corner. Dust from the gravel road swirled in a cloud behind her.

"He's still very tired, but the doctor says that's normal. How are you doing?" Aunt Lori sounded tired herself.

"I'm fine, busy, but things are going well. I'm on my way to take a stick out of a horse."

"Just another day at a vet practice," Aunt Lori said with a small laugh. "Uncle Alan asked me to remind Anita to do the supply checklist. He thinks the clinic is running low on—"

"You tell Uncle Alan that Anita has already sent in the order and everything at the clinic is under control." *Except my driving,* she thought, as she pushed the accelerator down, hoping she didn't hit any washboard on her way to the next call.

The Chapman ranch.

The last call she'd been on had taken too long. A sheep with trouble delivering her lambs. Something that could have been dealt with at the clinic, but the woman insisted someone come out to look at it.

Then the woman wanted her to check out her dog's gums and have a quick peek at her laying hens.

Which now meant that in spite of keeping the accelerator floored, she was twenty minutes late.

So it was easier to blame her heavily beating heart on the pressure of trying to get there on time rather than possibly seeing Nicholas again.

"But I gotta run, Aunty Lori. Tell Uncle Alan I'll be there tonight and give him a full report of how things are going."

"You take care, sweetie. I'll have supper ready for you when you come."

Cara smiled as she hung up. She was busy, sure, but there was a lot to be said for coming home after a hard day of work to supper cooking on the stove.

While she enjoyed cooking, many of her suppers back in Vancouver consisted of pizza or a bowl of cereal in front of the television. Hardly nutritious, despite the claims of the cereal manufacturers.

Cara made the last turn up the winding road leading to the ranch. She allowed herself a quick look at the mountains edging the fields. The bright spring sun turned the snowcapped peaks a brilliant white, creating a sharp relief against the achingly blue sky.

When she and Nicholas were dating, they seldom came to the ranch. This suited Cara just fine. Every time she came, she received the silent treatment from Nicholas's father, which created a heavy discomfort. Cara knew Nicholas's father didn't approve of her, though she was never exactly sure why.

All she knew was each time she saw Dale he glowered at her from beneath his heavy brows and said nothing at all.

So she and Nicholas usually went to a movie, hung out at her uncle and aunt's place or visited Nicholas's best friend, Lorne Hughes.

So when she found out the call came from Dale Chapman, she was already dreading the visit, and running late just made it more so.

She parked the car and, as she got out, she heard Dale Chapman speaking.

She grabbed a container with the supplies she thought she might need out of the trunk of the car. Then she headed around the barn to the corrals, following the sound of Mr. Chapman's voice.

Dale was holding the horse's head, talking in an unfamiliar gentle tone to his horse.

Just for a moment, Cara was caught unawares. She wasn't used to gentleness from Dale Chapman in any form.

"Good morning, Dale. Sorry I'm late."

His cowboy hat was pulled low on his head, shading his eyes, but when he looked up, his mouth was set in grim lines.

"I came as soon as I could." Cara knew trying to explain to him about unexpected problems with her previous case would be a waste of time.

Cara set the kit down in what seemed to be a safe place, pulled a pair of latex gloves out and slipped them on as she walked toward the horse.

She knew from the phone call that Dale had found the animal with a stick puncturing the muscles of its leg.

From here she could see the stick hanging down between his front legs. As she bent over to get a closer took, her mind skimmed frantically through her anatomy lessons, trying to picture which muscles the stick could have injured.

Watching the horse to gauge its reaction, she

gently touched the leg, feeling for heat. But he didn't flinch.

"When did this happen?" she asked, looking up at the wound. There was surprising little blood on the stick, which led her to believe it hadn't punctured anything important.

"Um…let's see…" Mr. Chapman hesitated, as if trying to recall.

"I found Duke this morning in the new pasture."

The deep voice behind her reverberated across her senses. Then Nicholas crouched down beside her and she caught the scent of hay and the faintest hint of soap and aftershave.

She couldn't stop the quick flashback to another time when she was at the ranch watching her uncle working on one of Nicholas's horses. It was the first time she met him.

Too easily she recalled how attracted she had been to him. And when his eyes had turned to her, the feeling of instant connection that had arced between them.

And right behind that came the memory of his father, watching her with narrowed eyes. *He still doesn't like me,* she thought, wondering once again why.

Not that it mattered. The way Nicholas acted around her, she was sure the son and the father were finally on the same page as far as she was concerned.

"Doesn't look like any veins or arteries are punctured," Cara said, gently touching the stick. It slid easily to one side. "I'm guessing it slipped between the muscles."

Duke shifted its weight and the stick moved down a bit more.

"I'm going to pull this out, but before I do, I want to give him some anesthetic," she said as she went back to the kit for a syringe and a needle. "How heavy is he—"

But as she spoke, Nicholas gave her the weight, as if anticipating her question.

She drew up the proper amount, pleased to see her hand held steady. She walked back to the horse but Nicholas was already at the Duke's head, brushing the mane back, giving her a clear injection site.

"Are you sure you should just pull that stick out?" Dale's voice said over her shoulder as she found a site for the needle. "That's going to be trouble."

"The stick is simply inserted between the sheaths housing the muscles. Pulling it out won't cause more problems."

Cara stifled her momentary irritation with Nicholas's father. When she had worked for her uncle before, she had occasionally encountered resistance from people who didn't think a woman was tough enough to do large animal work. And while she knew Nicholas's father never particularly cared for her, she didn't think that dislike extended to her capabilities as a vet.

"You haven't been doing this for a while—"

"I'll need a hose and water," Cara said, interrupting his questions. "Could you get that for me, Mr. Chapman?" she asked, gently tugging on the stick.

He grumbled a moment, but left, giving Cara room to breathe.

Cara eased the stick the rest of the way out, moving more carefully than she might have with someone else's horse, with someone else watching. She wanted to prove herself to Nicholas—to prove she wasn't as incompetent as his father seemed to think.

The stick came out without too much exertion. It was exactly as she had said. It had slipped between the muscles and had only punctured the skin.

"Thankfully the injury isn't major." She stood up and held out the stick to Nicholas, who took it from her without a word.

She got a large jug of distilled water and a bottle with a squirt cap from the car.

She gently ran her hands over the wound, then, pulling apart the skin, began to rinse. "I'm just doing an initial cleaning of the wound to make sure everything is okay," she said, intent on her task. "The rest will have to be done with a hose."

"Won't that be too cold?" Nicholas asked.

Cara shook her head, gently cleaning away a few bits of wood she had rinsed out of the wound. "The cold water will probably be soothing and help reduce any inflammation."

"And it will heal on its own? You're not going to stitch it up?"

"The wound needs to stay open so you can irrigate it. It will heal better that way."

"Really?"

"Are you questioning my abilities, as well?" she asked, as an edge entered her voice.

"What do you mean, 'as well'?"

Cara didn't reply. The words had spilled out in a wave of frustration with Mr. Chapman and Nicholas, but mostly with herself for her silly reactions to their presence.

"Duke is my father's favorite roping horse. You can't blame him for making sure he's being taken good care of." Nicholas frowned at her. He seemed surprised at her anger.

And he should be. When they were dating, she never lost her temper. She had always done what was expected. Been the one to keep the peace.

Fat lot of good that had done her.

Now, despite her simmering anger, she still couldn't break an age-old habit of avoiding confrontation, so instead of defending herself, she simply turned back to her patient and kept working.

"Here's the hose," Dale called out as he climbed over the corral fence. "You sure this will work?"

Cara didn't bother to answer. She just held her hand out for the end.

"You want to be careful with the angle of the hose. You don't want to be streaming the water directly upward into the wound," Cara said, demonstrating what she meant. "And keep the pressure low. You don't want to reinjure any regenerating tissue." She handed the hose to Nicholas and straightened, easing the crick out of her back.

"How will I know when I'm done?"

"Just do it for about ten minutes at a time. You'll also want to rinse the edges of the wound to keep it clean and to prevent it from scabbing over."

"It will never grow together." Dale planted his hands on his hips as if challenging her expertise. "You'll need to stitch it."

"I've seen a horse with a foot-long gash in its side that healed up on its own," Cara replied. "It's quite surprising how the body heals."

Dale didn't reply, and Cara hoped he was finished questioning and doubting her abilities.

She crouched down again, getting a closer look at what Nicholas was doing.

"Just keep doing that," she said, gently prying aside the skin. "I don't see any more bits of wood coming out and the water is running clean, so I think the bleeding has gone down."

She gently ran her hands down the leg, to double-check. "I'll give him some long-acting penicillin and I think that's all I need to do."

Nicholas stayed where he was and shot her a quick glance. As soon as their eyes met, she felt a lightness in her chest, as if someone had pulled her breath away.

Stop. Stop.

She caught her breath again, wishing her heart would settle down. How would she last until Gordon Moen, the new vet, came if a few glances from Nicholas could create such a strong reaction?

Cara closed the kit, latched it shut and drew a long, steadying breath, thankful she was just about done. "Do you have any more questions?"

Nicholas held her gaze and she saw a question in his eyes. It seemed as if he was going to say something, but then he drew back and shook his head. "If I do, I guess I can call the clinic."

She nodded, then turned away, surprised at a little flare of disappointment.

When she got to her car she was dismayed to see that Mr. Chapman had followed her.

"So you're all done?" he asked, staring at her from beneath his cowboy hat.

"The wound is clear and it looks like it should heal up just fine. I'll come by next week to double-check if I have time." Cara kept her tone professional. Detached, even, as she wondered why Dale had followed her.

Dale folded his arms over his chest, frowning. "He's over you, you know." His voice was quiet, determined. "He's started dating again."

She shouldn't care. Of course Nicholas would date again.

"That's good. I'm glad for him."

"He's got his own plans and his own life," he said, and though his voice had a threatening edge, as he spoke Cara caught the faintest note of desperation. Did he think she had any influence over his son's behavior?

"Again, I'm glad for him and you," she said, keeping her tone even. "Now if you'll excuse me, I have another call to make."

She pushed past him, her heart pounding with a variety of emotions. Frustration with Dale and her own silly reaction to Nicholas.

Too emotionally draining, she thought on the car ride back. Give it time.

She walked into the clinic and glanced at the clock as her stomach growled.

"Bill, you here?" she called out.

"He went out on a call," Anita replied from the front of the office. Anita came to the back of the clinic where Cara was replenishing her kit, wiping her hands on a towel.

"Did he say when he'd be back?"

"He had to go to Hunt's place and you know what a zoo that is."

"So, not until this afternoon." Cara sighed. Her workload just got heavier. She had a few appointments after lunch and she hoped no emergencies cropped up in the meantime.

Anita gave her an apologetic smile. "I know you've had a busy morning, but I have to run to the bank and deal with an overdraft. Do you mind covering the office for me?"

Cara didn't want to, but she didn't feel like telling Anita that. "If I get an emergency call, I'll have to call you back," Cara warned.

"Yeah. Sure." Anita flashed her a smile. "You're a dear. I'll make it up to you sometime."

Cara nodded as she closed the lid of the kit. Anita already owed her two lunch hours and a coffee break, but Cara wasn't about to get fussy about collecting on them. Once Gordon arrived, her job here was done.

Then, two minutes after Anita left, the buzzer to the front door sounded.

Of course, Cara thought, wiping her hands.

Trista Elderveld stood in the foyer, holding aloft two plastic bags and a tray of coffee. Her trim suit made her look far more professional and put together than Cara knew she actually was.

"Hey, girlfriend," Trista said with a quick grin. She put down the bags and coffee and gave her old friend a hug. "I'm so sorry to hear about your uncle."

Cara returned the hug. "Thanks. It's so good to see you again."

Trista pulled back and tugged at Cara's hair. "I like the longer length. Looks romantic."

"I was going for 'easier to care for,'" Cara said, deflecting Trista's loaded comment. "What do you have there?" she asked, pointing to the bags on the counter.

"Coffee and sub sandwiches from Hortons."

Cara's stomach groaned as she caught the scent of roasted onion. "You are a lifesaver. I just got back from a call at the Chapman ranch and thought I'd have to miss lunch."

"Really?" Trista angled her a curious glance. "And how did that go?"

"I was working. That's how it went." Cara's

stomach reminded her again that she hadn't eaten anything since the banana she gobbled down on the way to work this morning. "Why don't we go eat in my uncle's office so the front doesn't smell like a deli."

"Did you see Nicholas at all?" Trista asked as she followed Cara down the hall to the back office. "Did you talk to him? I heard he went to the hospital with you and your aunt."

"We're not talking about Nicholas, okay?" Cara said, keeping her tone firm, just in case Trista didn't get the hint.

"Changing subject, now." Trista unwrapped her sandwich. "How's your uncle doing?"

"He wants to come home already, but the doctor wants to keep an eye on him for a while."

"You doing okay, jumping back into large animal after treating puppies and guppies at your last job?" Trista asked with a grin.

"It's a nice change of pace." Cara took another bite and sighed with satisfaction. "No one makes sandwiches like Hortons. Thanks a bunch for doing this."

"I had an ulterior motive," Trista said, popping a pickle in her mouth. "I had stuff I needed to talk about without your aunt or uncle around. Anita told me Bill is gone on a call, so I hoped I could catch you alone."

"Sounds mysterious," Cara said, pushing an errant onion back between the slices of bread.

"Not so mysterious." Trista finished her sandwich, balled up the paper and tossed it in the garbage can. "I'm getting married."

Cara almost choked. "What? When?"

"A couple of weeks."

This time Cara did choke. Trista bounced across the room and pounded her friend on the back.

"What's the supersonic rush, girlfriend?" Cara gasped as she reached for her water bottle, struggling to gain her breath and composure.

Trista rubbed the side of her nose, then sighed. "Well, I'm pregnant."

Cara almost coughed again and was about to say something when her friend held up her hand.

"Before you say anything, you need to know that this isn't, well, wasn't a regular thing." Trista was blushing now and Cara was still speechless. "It just, well, happened. And we were talking about getting married anyway, so this just hurries up the process."

Cara sat back, still trying to absorb this information.

"Lorne's a great guy," Trista hastened to explain. "And I know he and Mandy used to be engaged, but that was different because she never liked his parents and they never really liked her."

Which sounded exactly like Nicholas's father, Cara thought.

"...but I love him and I know he loves me and I know we'll be happy together."

"That's good, I guess," Cara said, wishing she could be more enthusiastic about the situation.

Trista's smile trembled a moment and her eyes shone as if with tears. "I wish you could be happy for me. I know I'm happy in spite of how things are going."

Cara got up and gave her dear friend a quick hug. "If he makes you happy, then I'm happy for you."

"He will and he does," Trista said, her eyeblink releasing a tear. She brushed it away and sniffed lightly. "I love him more than I ever thought I could love someone, and he'll be a great husband and a fantastic dad."

Trista's enthusiastic defense of Lorne created a genuine smile in Cara.

Trista sniffed again, then looked back at Cara. "So now, I'm wondering how long you're sticking around?"

Cara felt a peculiar warmth as she guessed exactly where this was going. "I guess long enough to be at your wedding."

"So will you stand up for me at my wedding?"

Cara's smile blossomed. "Of course. For all the times you stood up for me when I first came here and for all the times you stuck up for me, yes, my dear friend, I will stand up for you."

Trista laughed aloud. "I'm so glad. You know your being here is an answer to prayer." Then a horrified look crossed her features and she held her hand up. "Not that I think your uncle's heart attack is an answer to prayer, but the fact that you're here and that you're not leaving and—"

"I know what you meant," Cara said with a melancholy smile as her own emotions veered from a tinge of jealousy to genuine pleasure. "And I would be honored to be your maid of honor."

Trista heaved a satisfied sigh. "I'm so, so glad. I know the wedding is sudden, but we both knew we wanted to get married and figured why waste time on a long engagement, which worked out perfectly because that means you're here for the wedding and everything seems to be falling into place…and I should stop talking so much, shouldn't I?" Trista gave a short laugh as she twirled a strand of hair around her finger. "You know I always talk a lot when I'm nervous and I was so worried you'd say no."

"Why would I do that?" Cara tossed her own

sandwich wrapper in the garbage can and leaned back to smile at her friend.

Trista flapped her hand, as if erasing the question. "Nothing. I'm just babbling."

"You can stop babbling. I will do all that is in my power to be the best maid of honor ever." Cara couldn't stop a quick glance at the clock, figuring she could spare Trista a few more minutes. After all, they had a wedding to plan.

"What's the first thing you need my help on?" Cara asked.

"Lorne and I decided we wanted an outdoor wedding so tomorrow night we're checking a place out."

"An outdoor wedding." Cara sighed, thinking of the plans she had made. Her plan had also been an outdoor wedding on a hill overlooking the mountains on Nicholas's ranch. "Where did you have in mind?"

Trista gave her hair another twirl. When she looked down, avoiding her gaze, a trickle of premonition chilled Cara's neck.

"Nicholas said we could get married at the ranch."

Her words fell like stones. No. She couldn't plan someone else's wedding at Nicholas's ranch.

"And one other thing," Trista said, clearing

her throat. "Lorne asked Nicholas to be his best man."

"Trista—"

"It's not a setup," Trista rushed to say. "Honestly. I knew you wouldn't be crazy about the idea and you can turn me down if you want, but I really, really could use your help and I want you to be my bridesmaid. Though you've been gone for a while, you're still my best friend. You're the only one who gets me." Trista sighed. "And you know how my mother is when she's flustered. She's no help at all and of all my high-school friends, you're the only one I stay in touch with and the only one who is organized enough to help me out."

Cara held Trista's earnest gaze while her practical nature fought with her rising emotions.

Trista had been her dearest friend since she moved to Cochrane. All through college and vet school, Trista was the only one Cara kept in contact with. It was Trista who had listened to her long-distance sorrow when Cara ran away from Nicholas.

If her friend wanted her help, then Cara knew she had to get past her own problems and do this.

"Okay. I'll be there."

"Tomorrow night. Eight o'clock. We're meeting at the ranch." Trista got up then gave Cara a hug. "I know this could be awkward, but hey, it's been three years and you're moving on, right? Like you told me?"

Cara nodded her agreement. She had to make Trista believe what she had told her all along. She was well and truly over Nicholas. "Of course I am. It will be fine."

But as she waved goodbye, her mind slipped back to that moment in the hospital when Nicholas had stood at her side at her uncle's bed.

Fine was too small a word to cover the emotions that could still grab her. She'd tried praying, but it was as if God, as He had before, didn't listen. Or didn't care.

You've got to take care of yourself, her mother's voice mocked her.

And you've got to guard your heart, her own memories told her.

Chapter Four

He's built a new shed, Cara thought as she took inventory of the main yard of Nicholas's ranch. And torn down the old one. The barn had gotten a new coat of paint and the fences of the corrals were painted, as well.

A faint breeze moved across the yard and Cara wrapped her thin sweater around her. Cara and her aunt had gone to the hospital to visit her uncle and as they were heading home Cara finally mentioned where she was going afterward.

She'd seen the questions in her aunt's eyes, but thankfully Aunt Lori said nothing.

Cara walked farther, her eyes moving from the buildings to the fields and pastures. The land, broken by swaths of evergreens, flowed upward to the blue-gray mountains with their jagged, snow-covered peaks guarding the ranch.

She'd seen the place for the first time when

her uncle came here to do a Cesarean on one of Nicholas's purebred cows. Cara came to assist and learn what she could. Uncle Alan had walked briskly toward the barn, a man intent on his work while she had dragged her feet, unable to look away from the craggy peaks capped with snow. She had wondered what it would be like to wake up every morning and see this breathtaking view.

And for a little while, when she and Nicholas were serious, the wondering moved toward reality.

Don't venture down that path, she reminded herself, pulling her thoughts back to the job at hand. *Stay in the present, the now.*

Cara glanced around the yard, dismayed to see that neither Trista nor Lorne had arrived.

She walked around the wooden fences of the corral, to see better, and as she did, the sound of hoofbeats caught her attention.

She looked toward the noise.

And her heart did a slow somersault.

A horse and rider moved toward her. Nicholas and Two Bits, she thought, recognizing the distinct blaze on the horse's dun face.

Nicholas had his cowboy hat pulled low over his face and he looked toward the mountains, as well, away from Cara. He held the reins loosely, moving easily with the chestnut horse as it cantered toward the corrals. Dust covered Nicholas's faded blue jeans. The tan shirt, with its cuffs rolled up, was also caked with dust.

Nicholas pulled Two Bits up short, then, with a subtle movement of his hands on the reins, turned his horse toward her. As horse and rider came near, Cara steeled herself. Seeing Nicholas on the horse, in his natural environment, resurrected a wave of nostalgia and unwelcome emotions.

Two Bits whinnied and Nicholas glanced up, a quick movement of his head.

In that moment, their eyes met and Cara felt it again.

That connection she thought she'd moved beyond. The attraction she thought she'd pushed aside.

"So, what brings you here?" he asked, pulling up beside her, curiosity edging his voice.

Had she come on the wrong day? Had she misunderstood?

"You come to check on Duke?" he continued.

"How is he?" she asked, seizing on the question as she tried to get her bearings.

"Good. I have to give him another shot tomorrow." Nicholas seemed to sense her puzzlement as he pushed his hat farther back on his head. "But you didn't come for Duke, did you?"

"Trista said we were meeting here to talk about

the wedding. Her and Lorne's wedding, that is." Cara clamped her mouth shut, angry at the flush staining her cheeks. She took a step back so she wouldn't have to crane her neck to look up at him.

Nicholas frowned, then, in one fluid motion, got off the horse. He pulled his hat off and hit it against his pants, releasing a cloud of dust. "Today?"

"That's what I understood." She was fairly sure she hadn't gotten the date wrong. Yesterday Trista had called her twice to confirm.

He ran his hand through his thick, dark hair, as if trying to dredge up the memory, his gray eyes looking confused. "I forgot completely about it."

Cara watched his hands, then swallowed, forcing herself not to take another step back.

"They're not here yet," Cara said, "but I'm pretty sure we had agreed to meet here today."

"And you came because you're the maid of honor," Nicholas said, a faint edge to his voice.

The hairs on the back of her neck rose up at his tone. "I hope that's not a problem?"

Nicholas shot her a frown. "Not unless it is for you."

"It's been three years. Long enough to have moved on," she said, thankful she sounded so casual and in control.

"And you have," Nicholas added.

His comment made it sound as if she had caused the breakup.

However, she could be an adult about this. She was only around for a while and then moving on.

"Looks like you've been busy with some improvements to the ranch," she said, striving for an airy tone of interest.

"Dad and I did a bunch of painting last time I was home. I'll have enough money to do some reno on the house when I come back from my next job."

Next job. A good reminder to Cara about where his priorities lay.

The growl of a diesel truck broke into the moment and with relief Cara looked around to see Trista clambering out of Lorne's truck.

"Hey there," she called, waving as she strode toward them. "Sorry we're late. Lorne had a flat tire on the way here."

Lorne, a tall, slender young man, his baseball cap shoved over dark hair, followed Trista, his walk an easy-going lope.

"Hey, bud," Lorne said, sending a grin Nicholas's way. "Were you out riding?"

Then before Nicholas could answer, Trista heaved a heavy sigh. "Don't tell me. You forgot."

Nicholas's gaze flicked from Trista to Lorne then back to Cara. "I did. Sorry."

"Honestly, Nicholas. How many messages do I have to send you?" Trista complained.

"I was out riding fences the past couple of days."

"I told your dad."

"I got the message. I just forgot. Sorry." Nicholas slapped his hat against his ripped pants, releasing another cloud of dust. "Give me twenty minutes."

"I'll put Two Bits away for you," Lorne said, taking the reins of the horse from his friend as he shot a frown at his friend. "You might want to rethink the wardrobe."

"Yeah, yeah. I'll be right back."

Trista shook her head as she watched Nicholas jog toward the farmhouse. "That guy never changes. This ranch is his everything, that's for sure."

Which was something Cara had to keep in mind if she wanted to keep her heart whole.

Ten minutes later, Two Bits was rolling on his back in the pasture with the other horses, looking ungainly and undignified but happy. Cara laughed at the sight.

Then Nicholas joined them, shoving the tails of his plaid shirt into his blue jeans.

"Sorry. Again," he said, pushing his still-damp

hair away from his face. A fan of pale lines radiated from his eyes, which were steel gray against his already tan skin. The eyes of a man used to squinting at the sun, looking out over pastures and hills.

"I know I forgot all about today, but I thought about the wedding and I had a few places in mind for the ceremony," Nicholas said, dropping a clean hat on his head. "One of them is close by, the other we'd have to drive to."

"Let's check the close one first," Trista said, pulling out a digital camera.

"It's over here. Past the barn and down the hill a bit."

As they walked through the yard, Cara felt a tremor of recognition, fairly sure they were headed to the same place she'd had in mind for her own wedding. The same place where Nicholas had proposed to her.

They headed around the barn, past a few tall pine trees and as they came into the open, Trista squealed with delight.

"This is perfect. Absolutely perfect," she said.

Cara followed, closing her mind off to her own memories, erasing the vision of herself standing on the grassy knoll overlooking a broad valley edged by trees flowing upward to the blue-peaked mountains.

"What do you think, Cara?" Trista exclaimed. "Isn't this gorgeous?"

"It is. Absolutely gorgeous," Cara said, looking out over the view, hoping Trista didn't catch the wistful tone in her voice.

She shot a quick glance at Nicholas, who was frowning at her, as if he had heard it. She held his gaze for a heartbeat, then her eyes slid back to the valley spread out below them. "You could put an arbor here with potted flowers tucked up against it," she said, walking to the edge of the hill. "That way you keep the view and you delineate the space for the ceremony."

"Oh, I like that," Trista said. "What kind of arbor?"

"Why not get your father to make one out of willows or something like that? You could buy some preplanted pots of flowers from the nursery and stagger them along the edges of the arbor and hang them from the top bar. Right about now they'd be clearing out their inventory and with a bit of pruning and repotting, they'd be in great shape by the wedding."

"I knew you'd be able to help me out," Trista said. "You seem to know exactly what to do."

That was only because, at one time, these ideas had been for her own wedding.

"We could rent chairs from the church," Cara added, walking slowly around the open area, gently teasing out her own memories, her old plans. "We can hang some pots on shepherd hooks stuck in the dirt beside the chairs. Sort of like living pew markers."

"You are so good at this," Trista said with a satisfied note in her voice. "I knew I got the right person when I asked you."

"The grass will need to be mowed," Nicholas said, "and I'll need help setting everything up."

"I could get my brothers to come out and help with all that stuff," Lorne said.

"Who is doing the service?" Cara asked.

Trista pulled a small book out of her purse. "Pastor Samuels said he'd be willing to do the service, but he wants to meet with us a couple of times before the wedding."

"I still think we should check out the church and that hall my mom was talking about," said Lorne.

Cara frowned. "But I thought having the wedding here was—"

"Lorne's mom wants a church wedding," said Trista.

"She just said it would be easier," Lorne said, his tone becoming defensive.

"Everyone has their wedding at a church and their reception at a hall. I don't want to be everyone."

Lorne tugged on the brim of his hat with a

jerky motion. "And she thinks that not getting married in a church is like admitting—"

"That we made a mistake?" Trista's voice rose a notch and Cara felt their tension from here.

Obviously the bride and groom needed some space, so Cara walked to the edge of the knoll and wrapped her arms around herself as she looked out over the valley.

Below her, a dirt road snaked along the edge of the fenced field, then disappeared into a cut in the hills.

She knew the road led to the higher pastures where the cows were grazing. She had never been there, but every time Nicholas talked about the high pastures, his voice grew quiet with reverence.

Then the hairs on the back of her neck bristled and she didn't need to look around to know Nicholas stood right behind her.

How, after all this time, could she still be so aware of him? And why was he seeking her out?

The longer he stood there, the more aware of him she became.

"I was wondering how Alan was doing?" he finally asked, his voice quiet. "I meant to go and visit, but I had too much to do here."

Her mind cast back to that moment they had shared as they stood beside her uncle's bedside.

How she had leaned against him and allowed him to support her.

That had been a mistake. In the past few years she had learned that while one may be the loneliest number, it was also the safest.

Cara felt the silvery flash of the beginnings of a headache. The week had been too busy, she thought. She'd had too much on her mind—that was why she felt so vulnerable.

"He's doing okay," she said. "The doctor said he could come home tomorrow. I'm hoping to visit him tonight."

"I'm glad he's okay. Must be hard on your aunt."

Cara thought of Aunt Lori's quiet stoicism, which almost cut her more than any fussing and fretting would have.

"She's concerned, of course," Cara said. "But we're both very thankful he's doing so well."

"And the clinic?"

"He won't be able to return to work full-time for a while."

"I heard he and Bill had a new vet coming?"

Cara nodded, her eyes still staring sightlessly at the view below her. "He's not here for another three weeks."

"And you're staying until then?"

Was she imagining the faint hint of disappointment in his voice? Or was she simply projecting her own misgivings onto him?

Had he missed her? Had he thought of her after she left?

"I'll have to. I can't go to Europe knowing that Uncle Alan can't work."

"I hope he can get back to it soon," Nicholas said. "It would be a shame if he has to slow down. He enjoys his work."

"He must," Cara said, shooting Nicholas a quick glance. "He's been here forever."

"You sound surprised."

"I can't imagine what it's like to be tied down to one place," she said, hoping her wistful feelings didn't enter her voice.

His eyes narrowed and she didn't imagine the frown shoving his eyebrows together. "No. I didn't think you could."

She caught a note of anger threading through his voice and then he turned and walked away from her.

He had misunderstood her.

And she knew he saw her the way his father did. Rootless. Unwilling to commit. The thought kindled her anger. She wouldn't have said yes to marrying him if that was the case, but if he couldn't see that, then she couldn't change his opinion of him now.

Just as well, she thought, turning back to the

scenery in front of her. Anger was an easier emotion to sustain around Nicholas than the yearning winding around her heart each time she saw him.

Cara waited a moment, then followed him to where Trista and Lorne were still talking, hoping she could sustain her emotional distance from him over the next while.

"I don't think we need to look at the other place," Trista was saying, her smile as bright as the summer sun shining down on them. "Lorne agrees with having the wedding here. This is the perfect spot. We've got lots of room for guests to park and the view is stunning." Trista flashed a grin at Cara. "What do you think?"

"If you two agree on it," she said.

"My mom will just have to get over the fact that we aren't having a church wedding," Lorne said. It looked as if their differences had been ironed out. "If this is what Trista wants, then that's good enough for me." Lorne looked down at Trista with such love and devotion that Cara's heart faltered at the sight.

They looked so happy and Cara knew she had to set her own feelings aside for the sake of her close friend's happiness.

Trista released a sigh of satisfaction as she tucked her arm into Lorne's. "I can't thank you enough, Nicholas, for suggesting this. It's absolutely perfect for a wedding."

"Yeah, I thought so, too," Nicholas said.

"And I want to let you know that my mom and dad are putting on an engagement party for us at our house on Saturday," Trista said. "We'd like you two to come."

You two. As if they were still a couple.

"I'll be there," Cara said just as her phone started to buzz. Cara pulled it out and glanced at the number on her screen.

"Sorry, people, I gotta go," she said.

"Is it your uncle?" Nicholas asked, his concern giving her a surprising lift.

"No. It's a vet call." She gave him a tight smile, then walked swiftly to her car, as if outrunning her own emotions.

Chapter Five

The Elderveld place was a zoo, Nicholas thought, watching the aimless movement of bodies from the house to the decorated yard. Minilights twinkled from the branches of the shrubs and trees surrounding the large front lawn. Tables and stacks of chairs filled one corner of the yard. Some older women were directing the movements, contradicting each other from the sounds of the complaints being registered by the men by the chairs.

He waited a moment before descending into the chaos, catching his breath from his mad drive over. His hair was still damp from the quick shower he'd taken to wash off any hay dust that had accumulated while he'd been swathing the hayfields.

Thankfully he'd gotten all the hay cut. But just barely.

"Are you sure you want the cake out yet?" one female voice called out.

"What do I do with the fruit platter?"

"If I get asked one more question I'm going to scream," Trista's mother called from inside the house. "When is Cara coming?"

The sound of her name made him take another breath.

He felt as if he teetered on the edge of an unpredictable wave that had the potential to swamp him. And it wasn't the number of people milling around the yard or the decibel level that bothered him.

Cara was going to be here.

The other day on the ranch, he'd caught a hint of their old relationship, of that unusual rapport he and Cara shared from their first "hello."

And he realized that he had missed her.

She's not staying. She's leaving as soon as she can, he reminded himself.

And if he wanted to move on, he had to get used to seeing her and keep old emotions from clouding his judgment. She wasn't a part of his life or his life's plan anymore.

Nicholas took a breath and headed toward the yard just as one of Trista's teenage sisters came stomping down the sidewalk toward him. Her T-shirt was a neon storm, matching the flurry of color in her hair, and her blue jeans were ripped at the knees. "I'm not changing," she yelled. "You have to take me as I am." Then she looked ahead and her bright-pink eyelids narrowed over her eyes.

"What are you staring at, mister?" she snapped.

"Nothing," he said, feeling intimidated by her strident teenage attitude.

"Like the shirt, Twyla."

Though the voice behind him was quiet, the sound gave him an unwelcome jolt.

"Hey, Cara, about time you came," Twyla said, her voice holding the faintest note of insolence.

"Hey, yourself. Why are you smart-mouthing Mr. Chapman?" Cara now stood beside him, facing down the impudent young girl.

Today her hair hung loose, a golden cloud that rested on her narrow shoulders. She wore a flowing kind of sweater over a pink tank top, strung with a couple of necklaces, and slim blue jeans.

She looked amazing.

Twyla folded her skinny arms over her equally skinny waist, ignoring Cara as her gaze slipped up and down Nicholas as if inspecting him. "Is this Nicholas, Uncle Lorne's best man?"

"Yes. He is."

Twyla's eyes took on a peculiar glint. "He's pretty hot. Trista said you used to date him," she said, sounding catty. "Why did you dump him?"

Despite his decision to act casual, Nicholas couldn't stop the sideways slide of his gaze toward Cara, wondering what she was going to say.

"This isn't a reality television show, so I don't have to tell you." Cara gave her a quick smile.

Twyla rolled her eyes and strolled away, leaving Nicholas and Cara by themselves.

"So, I guess we're supposed to help out with this thing," Nicholas said, hoping he sounded cool and composed. "Do you have any idea what we're doing?"

"Trista told me to show up early, that's all I know."

Nicholas pushed his cowboy hat back on his head as he glanced around the chaos of the yard. Mr. Elderveld was talking to Mr. Hughes. Lorne and his brothers were leaning on a stack of chairs, laughing. And from the house, Nicholas could hear more complaining.

"I'm getting nervous about this wedding," Nicholas said.

"Has Trista talked to you about any of her plans?"

"Other than the fact that they're getting married on the yard, no. And Lorne keeps telling me Trista is in charge. He's a great guy, but he keeps talking about letting go and trusting, which doesn't make for good wedding planning."

"You're taking this pretty seriously," Cara said with a light laugh.

"Marriage is serious," he said.

She caught a faint undercurrent and wondered if he was referring to his mother. Or her.

Cara pushed out her lower lip and blew out her breath. "I'm worried Trista has taken too much on. I don't know how she'll pull all this together in the time they have left."

"Lorne doesn't even know how many people they're inviting."

"I guess I'll have to help her a bit more."

"You don't have time for that, do you?"

"I owe Trista a lot, so for her, I'll make time."

"I'll have to make time, too. That wedding is taking place on my yard and I don't want a fiasco on my hands."

"Fair enough." She gave a delicate shrug of her shoulder. "So what do you want to do?"

"I'd like to get together tomorrow with Lorne and Trista and make a few plans," Nicholas said.

He didn't imagine her slight withdrawal, and he wondered if he shouldn't have offered to help. But what could he do?

It was either get involved or have potential

chaos on his hands and on his ranch in a couple of weeks.

Neither option was great.

Then Cara nodded. "That'd be good. Bill is on call tomorrow."

"So we'll talk more then."

He could tell she wasn't crazy about the idea either. That didn't matter to him. There was no way he was having a disorganized wedding at his place.

"Hey. Chapman. Over here." Lorne was calling him.

"I gotta go," Nicholas said, jutting his chin in Lorne's direction.

"Let me know what time you want me there tomorrow."

"Come after church," he said. His father would be at some horse clinic that day, so it would be safest to have everyone come then.

Then he turned and walked over to where his friend stood chatting with his brothers. Lorne winked at Nicholas when he came near.

"So, I saw you talking with Cara?"

Nicholas gave him a dry look. "Yeah. What of it?"

Lorne held his hands up. "I'm guessing...you're still ticked at her?"

"I'm guessing people will get hungry soon so we should start putting chairs out."

"Oh, yeah." Lorne looked at his watch. "Looks like we are running a bit late."

"Why don't you get your brothers to put out the tables, and we can put chairs around them. The women will want to put cloths on them or some such thing."

Lorne shrugged. "Who knows."

Nicholas shook his head and started unstacking the first set of chairs. But as he worked and against his will, Nicholas glanced over his shoulder and each time he saw Cara organizing things on her end.

Lorne caught the direction of his gaze, frowned, and drew Nicholas aside by the shoulder. "Are you sure you're okay with this? I mean, with Cara and all?"

Nicholas forced a laugh. "It's over, Lorne. Has been for three years."

Lorne shrugged. "Maybe, but I know you cared about her and I didn't get the whole attraction thing until I met Trista. If what you had with Cara was anything like what I have with Trista—"

"If what I had with Cara was the same, we would have been married already," Nicholas said, unable to keep the sharp note out of his voice.

"But it's still gotta be hard to see her like this. I told Trista she had to ask someone else, but she wouldn't and neither would I, so here you two are. Stuck with seeing each other. Sorry."

Nicholas shrugged. "I'll deal. It's sort of like that horse I used to have. The one that spooked every time something brushed its stomach."

"I remember the time he dumped you in the patch of thistles," Lorne said with a laugh. "But I don't get the Cara connection."

"Remember how I fixed the problem?"

Lorne nodded, but still looked puzzled.

"I took it in the corral. Brushed it with sticks and sacks and my hand and kept at it until it got desensitized. Until it didn't jump each time it saw a stick or something coming at it." Nicholas lifted one shoulder in a slow shrug. "I just have to do the same with Cara. Get desensitized."

Lorne nodded slowly, as if he didn't quite get it but was willing to go along with the idea. "Desensitized. Sure. Whatever."

"And the more I see her, the less spooked I'll get."

"Just make sure you don't get spooked the day of my wedding."

"I'll be there." Nicholas slapped his friend on the shoulder. "Now let's finish with those chairs before the women start nagging. Then we can get going on those lanterns I see piled by the trees."

Half an hour later, chaos had fled and order

had been restored and Mr. Elderveld was calling out for people's attention. Both sets of parents of the bride and groom stood side by side, fidgeting and tossing quick glances at each other.

Nicholas knew Lorne's mother, Mrs. Hughes, hated fuss and hated being the center of attention. Yet there she stood in her party clothes, smiling at her son and Trista, who sat at a table beside them.

"We'd like to thank everyone for coming here," Mr. Elderveld was saying once the noise settled down. "I'm hoping the weather for the wedding is as cooperative as it has been for this party." He glanced down at his daughter and gave her a loving smile. "I'm so thankful we can celebrate this special occasion and though I know the wedding is only a couple of weeks away, we wanted to do things right and in this family that means we have an engagement dinner." He glanced over at Lorne's father. "I'd now like to ask Mr. Hughes to say a blessing on the food."

Lorne's father stepped forward. "My wife and I would like to thank Mr. and Mrs. Elderveld for hosting this party. This means a lot." Mr. Hughes tucked his hands in the back pockets of his pants, glancing at his son and future daughter-in-law. "We all know this is a difficult situation for you two, but we want to show you that we support you both and are thankful you are taking this step.

You are a blessing to us from the Lord in so many ways. Your future wedding is a celebration and, as Mr. Elderveld said, this engagement dinner is part of that." He paused a moment, glancing around the crowd as if making sure everyone there understood. "Now if you could all bow your heads, I'll ask God for a blessing on this evening and on the bridal couple and their future plans."

As Mr. Hughes spoke, a peculiar sensation curled through Nicholas's midsection.

He thought of his own father. Dale Chapman had openly struggled with his feelings toward Cara. How would he have reacted had the two of them been in the same situation as Lorne and Trista?

Would he have been as supportive? As encouraging?

Would he have been able to thank the Lord for them and to pronounce a blessing on their plans?

The thought settled, creating a restless current of uncertainty.

Was his father one of the unspoken reasons Cara had left?

Nicholas knew exactly where Cara was and he chanced a quick glance her way.

Cara was looking at Trista and her face was etched with a sorrow so strong Nicholas had to fight the urge to go to her, put his arms around her and hold her close.

And he wondered what, exactly, had created her sadness.

Cara swiped at her eyes and before she bowed her head, she looked over at him, as well.

Their gazes met and eyes held and it seemed as if time slipped backward. As if the angry words spoken about the ranch and his risky work—her sudden disappearance and long silence afterward—as if none of that had happened.

Because in that moment, awareness, as tangible as a touch, arced between them and everyone around them faded away.

For that moment it was just he and Cara as time hovered.

Then Cara jerked her head to the side, breaking the connection.

And as she did, Nicholas knew that putting his relationship with Cara behind him was going to be harder than he thought.

Just get through it. Just get through this wedding stuff and then both of you will be going your separate ways. She to Montreal and you to Kuwait.

The thought depressed him, but he pushed it aside. The ranch was doing well, but every bit of money he made brought it further along.

When everything was exactly the way

he wanted, then he would quit and ranch full-time.

And he hoped, when that happened, he was going to find someone he could love as he once loved Cara.

Chapter Six

"It's good to be home." Alan sat back in his chair, glancing around the living room with a satisfied sigh. "I can't believe it's been a week already."

To Cara, he still looked pale. And his shirt and jacket hung on his large frame. She stacked up the old magazines that had gathered on the couch and added them to the pile of newspapers she had put on the coffee table.

"And everything is still okay at the clinic?" he asked Cara. "Do you need me to stop in?"

"Everything is still under control. Don't you dare drop in," Cara said, snapping open a garbage bag. "You need to rest."

"Like you're resting?" he teased as she dumped the magazines in the bag.

"I'm not the one who had a heart attack."

"You might get one the way you've been going.

You haven't sat down since I came home," he said. "Just relax."

But Cara couldn't. When she came back from the hospital she had immediately started tidying. She'd made some progress, but she'd had to ignore the disorganized pantry. She would have loved to tackle the kitchen, but her aunt was there now, making up a snack for them.

"I want to get a little more done before I go," she said, tying the handles of the garbage bag.

Uncle Alan caught her hand as she bent over to pick up the discarded coffee cup from the floor beside him. "You didn't want to go to church with your aunt? You could have easily picked me up afterward."

Cara didn't meet her uncle's eye, feeling a nudge of guilt at the concern she saw there. "No. I…wanted to get you home as soon as they released you." That was a lame response, but it was mostly the truth. She didn't want to tell him that last week she'd felt uncomfortable singing songs about drawing closer to Jesus and about trusting in Him.

She preferred to trust in herself. Just as her mother had always taught her. She realized the benefits of that now. There were fewer disappointments in your life when you didn't count on others for happiness. Love was too risky. Either love of God or love of others. They required too much trust and that trust was too often broken.

"I don't mind being home earlier. I get tired pretty quick. It's frustrating," he said.

Cara curled her hand around his, squeezing it gently. "You don't have to worry about anything. The clinic is doing fine."

"I'm trying not to worry," Alan said, shifting in his chair. "But the doctor says I'll be back at work soon," he said, returning Cara's hand squeeze.

Cara didn't reply because she knew better. The specialist had been fairly emphatic about Uncle Alan making drastic changes in his lifestyle.

And the most drastic had to do with his work. He was too old to deal with the stress of late-night calls, which meant his work would slow considerably.

"Have you talked to that new vet, Gordon?" Cara asked. "Is there any way he can come sooner?"

"I called him and he said he might. Depending on how things go with the job he's working now."

"So are you ready for dessert?" Aunt Lori asked, coming into the living room, carrying a tray of fruit and three small bowls.

Uncle Alan pulled a face at the fruit and Cara stifled a smile. Uncle Alan loved his sweets and she could see future battles with her aunt once he felt better.

She glanced at the clock, then got to her feet, grabbing the garbage bag as she left. "Sorry to bail on you, but I have to meet Nicholas."

Uncle Alan's frown made her smile.

"We're planning Lorne and Trista's wedding," she assured him. "They'll be there, as well."

He relaxed visibly. "Okay then. You go."

Cara brushed a kiss over his forehead. "And you make sure you take care of yourself."

But as she straightened, he caught her by the hand, squeezing it as if to catch her attention.

"And you take care of yourself, too," he said, his serious voice holding another undertone.

"I will."

But as she got into her uncle's car, his warning rang in her ears.

Uncle Alan knew exactly the struggle Cara had with Nicholas. It was he who had told her sometimes hard choices needed to be made and that it wasn't wrong to think of herself. Uncle Alan knew better than anyone else how much Cara had been hurt by her mother's decisions and by her mother's choices. And it was he who had held a sobbing Cara in his arms when she had come back from Nicholas's ranch, after breaking up with him.

And now she was heading right back there.

She had changed, she thought as she turned onto the road leading to the ranch. Her heart wasn't as easily ensnared. She'd been on her own for three years and had developed some independence and a tougher crust.

But as she parked her car beside Lorne's truck, she couldn't stop the fluttering of that supposedly free heart.

Remnants of old emotions, she told herself as she got out.

"Hey, Cara, over here," she heard Lorne's voice calling out from beyond the barn.

Frowning, Cara walked in the direction of his voice. What were they doing at the corrals?

She came around the corner. Lorne was stroking one of Nicholas's horses and grinned up at her when she came closer.

"I thought we could go for a ride up into the mountains after our meeting," Lorne said.

"Where's Trista?"

"She and Nicholas are in the barn, checking out if it's big enough for the wedding reception in case we have rain."

"So if we go with a barbecue, we could do it standing up," Trista was saying as she and Nicholas came out of the barn. Then she glanced over and saw Cara. "You're here. Thank goodness."

And Cara didn't imagine the look of relief on her friend's face.

"So why don't we go to the house and get a few things set out," Cara said.

"What's to talk about?" Lorne said. "We got the place, we got the minister, the other things can wait—"

"No, they can't," Nicholas said. "And Trista's been taking care of the other things all on her own." The slightly angry tone of his voice surprised Cara. He was taking this wedding seriously.

Which created a lingering, twisted pain. Had he shown as much commitment to their relationship, things might have been so different.

She pushed the feelings aside.

"Before we head up into the mountains, lovely though that may be, we need to do some basic planning," Cara said, underlining Nicholas's opinion.

Lorne glanced at Trista, and then, thankfully gave a light shrug. "Okay. If that's what you think should happen."

"As the maid of honor, I do."

As Cara spoke, she caught Nicholas's relieved gaze. And then a smile.

As she returned it, a sense of equilibrium returned. It was going to be okay. *I'll get through this just fine. We're just two old acquaintances helping friends plan a wedding. Nothing more.*

"We can go up to the house and work there,"

Nicholas said, leading the way. "Dad's gone so it will be quiet."

As Cara followed, she looked behind her at the beckoning mountains, feeling a moment of kinship with Lorne. The sun was shining and she had some time off, so she would much sooner have ridden up into the mountains than sit inside and plan a wedding that should have been hers.

The past year, in her last job, most of her work had been inside, working with small animals. She had often thought of the wide-open spaces of Alberta when she was casting broken limbs and stitching and dosing in the confines of the vet office.

She pushed the yearning aside.

If she was going to be a part of this wedding she couldn't let it just "happen" as Lorne seemed to think it would. For Trista's sake, she needed to help.

"Sorry about the mess," Nicholas was saying as she stepped into the kitchen.

Cara blinked. Mess? All she saw were some coffee cups on the table and a couple of magazines.

If Nicholas truly wanted to see a mess, he should come to her aunt's place.

This kitchen, though showing signs of age, was clean and tidy. The countertop gleamed and the stove shone. The old wooden table, though scarred and worn, held a ceramic bowl with a bunch of apples.

Cara's mind flashed back to the modern, expensive furniture filling her aunt and uncle's home. The money, which was no problem for Aunt Lori and Uncle Alan, couldn't replicate the homey comfort of this worn but clean kitchen.

This could have been mine, she thought, the idea lacerating her hard-won composure.

Cara pressed her lips together and marshaled her defenses. Over. Past.

She pulled a wooden chair back from the table, dropped into it and pulled out a pad of paper from the briefcase she had taken along.

And then, almost against her will, she glanced in Nicholas's direction.

He wore an old shirt, his sleeves rolled up as he measured coffee grounds into a coffee press. While she watched he rinsed a cloth and wiped the already clean counters. He poured boiling water into the press, set out cups, found a plate in the cupboard and a bag of cookies and put that out, as well.

She tried to imagine her uncle working as efficiently in her aunt's kitchen. The picture didn't gel.

Lorne and Trista were huddled together, whispering and giggling like a couple of teenagers, their previous tiff obviously forgotten. Cara cleared her throat to get their attention. "So how many people will be coming?" she asked.

Trista pulled away from Lorne, then bent over, pulling a folder out of a bag she had taken along. "We're keeping it small. Just family and close friends."

"And how many is that?" Cara asked. As Nicholas set her mug in front of her, she noticed he had put cream in it. Just enough to give it a faint caramel color. He remembered, she thought, the idea giving her heart a silly lift.

Old acquaintances. That's all.

"Not sure," Lorne said.

"Let's see your list?" Cara asked. Trista handed her a paper from the folder.

"We don't really have time to send things out in the regular mail," Trista said, "so I thought we could e-mail whoever has an e-mail address and phone the people who don't."

"So how many people would that be?" Nicholas asked as he sat in an empty chair beside Cara. She caught the scent of his cologne and the faintest hint of hay and straw from the barn, and she noticed the silvery line of a scar along his forearm that she didn't remember being there before.

An accident at work? Or at the ranch?

Focus, you silly girl.

"About sixty, we guessed?" Lorne said.

"I'd like to ask some girls from work," Trista said.

Lorne frowned. "I thought we were keeping the wedding small."

"Well, yeah, but I've worked with them for the past four years—"

"Then I should ask some friends from my work, too," Lorne put in.

"Of course," Trista said.

"So that makes it, what, eighty now?" Cara wrote the number down at the top of page one.

"Only if my brothers don't bring escorts," Lorne added.

Cara couldn't help a quick glance at Nicholas, who was rolling his eyes.

"Let's get a firm list down now. Trista, you send out the e-mails as soon as possible and give people a week to reply," Cara said, feeling like a schoolteacher. "Then we'll follow up with the people we haven't heard from. In the meantime we need to think about the meal."

"Nicholas suggested we have a barbecue," Lorne said. "Do it ourselves. Get the relatives to all bring something—like a bit of a potluck."

Cara stifled a groan and chanced a look at Nicholas. "Did you suggest that?"

Nicholas shrugged, looking a bit baffled himself. "I did, when we were talking about only thirty people."

Cara imagined herself, in her bridesmaid dress, whipping up a taco salad between the ceremony and dinner. "I think if we can get someone else to do the meal, we should definitely look at that." She made another quick note.

An hour and a half later they had a list of people who would be attending, a tentative plan for the service and a rough concept of how Trista wanted the yard decorated and set up.

"So, is that good enough for now?" Lorne asked, shifting in his chair.

"What about the supper menu?"

Lorne blew out his breath and got up. "If you're getting a caterer, they can take care of that, can't they?"

Cara bit back a sigh and chanced a look at Nicholas, who was rolling his eyes again. Then their gazes caught and she let slip a smile of commiseration.

"We live a ways out of town for a caterer to come," Nicholas said. "We could get one of those people with a portable barbecue thing."

"Sounds good." Lorne looked relieved.

"It's a bit casual," Nicholas warned.

"Casual is what we're going for, right, babe?" Lorne said, with a wink in Trista's direction.

She smiled back, nodding. "Yeah. But I still want it nice."

"It will be nice," Lorne said. "Nice and easy."

He glanced from Cara to Nicholas. "So what else do we need to talk about?"

"The ceremony?" Cara asked.

"We're meeting with the minister on Tuesday."

"Sound system?" Nicholas put in.

"My brother has one. From his band days."

Lorne seemed to have an answer for everything, Cara thought, but his remarks were so glib and offhand. As if he were simply going through the motions of planning this wedding so he could get on to other things.

"And photographer?"

"That's why I wanted to go riding," Lorne said. "So we could find a place to take pictures. I don't want the usual studio stuff."

"But you'd have to bring the photographer out there, too," Cara said, puzzled at his insistence that they go out on horses to find the perfect spot, when there were some equally lovely places here on the ranch.

"That's fine," Trista added, seemingly okay with the plan. "The photographer suggested it himself when he found out where we were having the wedding."

"So you're good with all of this?" Cara asked.

Trista nodded, but Cara could see faint lines of tension around her mouth.

"Then I think we got everything we need," Cara said, sensing her friend needed a break. "I guess you guys can go look for your picture spot."

"I want you to come, too," Trista said to Cara.

"Why?" Cara hadn't figured on that.

"I need your advice. Maid of honor, remember?" Trista tossed Cara a pleading look.

Cara remembered another time she had gone riding with Nicholas. They had ridden up into the mountains and had a picnic overlooking a lake nestled in the valley. And had shared numerous kisses, which had more than made up for the slight fear she had felt while riding. She loved working with horses on the ground, not so much in the saddle.

"I don't think—"

Trista cut of her protest. "Please come. Please?"

Cara pushed down the memory of the kisses, avoiding looking at Nicholas for fear he would notice the flush in her cheeks.

"Okay. I guess I can come," she conceded, sensing Trista needed the emotional support.

"Are you sure we got everything covered?" Nicholas asked.

"We can talk a bit more on the ride if we need to," Cara said.

"Lorne and I will get the horses ready then," Nicholas said, getting up from the table. "So you're coming riding?" Nicholas glanced at Cara.

She nodded, wondering if she would regret doing this.

"That's great. I'll saddle up Two Bits," he said, a smile teasing one corner of his mouth. "You'll be okay on him."

"I hope so," she said.

"You can trust him."

She knew he was talking about the horse, yet sensed an underlying meaning that created a tiny frisson of expectation.

"You coming, Chapman?" Lorne called out from the porch.

"Trista and I will clean up," Cara said, gathering up the mugs.

Nicholas held her gaze a split second longer than necessary and then left.

Trista was already filling the sink with water, staring out the window overlooking the yard. Cara could see Lorne and Nicholas walking toward the corral, Nicholas's long strides easily catching up to Lorne. It looked as if he could be talking to Lorne and Cara hoped, for Trista's sake, he was asking him about his offhand treatment of this wedding.

Because the frown on Trista's face ignited Cara's concern.

"Is everything okay?" Cara gently asked.

Trista tugged her gaze away from the men and gave Cara a quick smile. "Yeah. Just feeling a bit confused."

"Over the wedding?"

Trista turned off the taps and dropped the mugs into the soapy water. "A bit."

"And how about Lorne. How does he feel about it all?"

"He's just…well…he doesn't like all this planning stuff."

"Does he like all this marrying stuff?" Cara slowly wiped a mug, wishing she knew how to proceed.

"Of course he does. Lorne loves me."

Cara didn't imagine the tone of indignation in Trista's voice, but behind that she also heard a hint of fear.

"I'm sure he does." Cara fought her own urge to caution her friend. But she knew she had to talk to Nicholas later. Find out if he knew what was going on with Lorne.

"And if you're insinuating he's only marrying me because I'm pregnant—"

"No. I'm not." Cara caught Trista by the shoulder, concerned by the sparkle of tears in Trista's eyes. "I just…I just want to make sure everything is okay with you two."

Trista swiped her eyes and gave Cara a trembling smile. "This pregnancy is making me really weepy and emotional and I'd be lying if I said I didn't feel overwhelmed."

"Let me take care of some of this," Cara urged.

Trista sniffed. "I can't do that. You've got enough going on—"

"Tell me what still needs to be done," Cara urged. "I want to help."

Trista sighed. "The cake needs to be done. Mom's sister was going to bake it, but she's not feeling well and begged off. I loved your idea about the buckets of flowers, and the nursery is clearing out their stock this week but I don't have time to go get the plants and take care of them. And I need to figure out if I want to put something on the tables." Then she sniffed again. "I just feel like it's all getting to be too big and too much."

Cara thought of her own busy schedule, but then looked at Trista's face and made a quick decision. "Tell you what. Aunt Lori and I will take care of the cake. I'll go to the nursery this week and pick up the plants."

"That's too much—"

"No. It isn't. Things are getting a bit quieter

at the clinic and I know Aunt Lori would love to help out." Cara gave her friend a quick smile. "And if we get Uncle Alan to water the flowers every day he'll have something to do, as well."

Trista looked down at the soap bubbles clinging to her hands. "That would be great."

Cara wiped the last mug and set it on the counter. "We're done here, so let's go outside and enjoy this beautiful day," Cara said, hanging the dish towel on the bar of the oven, glancing around the tidy kitchen with the smallest flicker of envy. This place seemed more like a home in some ways than her own uncle and aunt's place.

By the time Cara and Trista joined the men, the horses were saddled and ready.

The sun's warmth surrounded them, the air held a soft breeze and as Cara looked up, a flock of sparrows swooped and played on the wind. A perfect day for a ride.

"You should shoot those things," Lorne was saying, looking up at the sparrows. "You've got tons of them."

"They don't bother me, I don't bother them." Nicholas laughed.

Lorne saw the girls and grinned. "Let's get going," Lorne said, looking and sounding a lot more cheerful than he had inside the house.

He helped Trista into the saddle and as he

adjusted her stirrups, he was laughing up at her and smiling as if everything were fine.

And maybe it was, Cara thought.

Nicholas stood holding Two Bits, another horse tied up to the fence behind him.

"So you ready to go?" he asked, leading Two Bits toward her.

Cara looked at the huge chestnut with some trepidation. The one time she had gone riding with Nicholas, she had been on a much smaller horse, a mare named Blossom. Nicholas had ridden Two Bits and his horse had dwarfed Cara and her mount. But she'd felt quite at ease not being so far from the ground.

"He's a great horse. I trust him with my life," Nicholas said by way of encouragement. "And, more important, I trust him with yours."

Thus assured she stretched up to grasp the pommel but couldn't lift her leg high enough to reach the stirrup. Then before she could think of how to solve this, Nicholas had her foot in his hand, his other hand on her waist and he lifted her easily up.

Cara fussed needlessly with the reins, hiding the twinge of pleasure his touch gave her.

"Looks like Lorne and Trista are eager to be off," Nicholas said, untying the other horse and swinging easily into the saddle.

"Do they know where to go?" Cara asked, as

they disappeared into the trees crowding the trail they were following.

"Lorne knows the place." Nicholas glanced her way, frowning. "You okay?"

"Yeah. I'm fine." But as she chanced a look down, *fine* was replaced by a quiver of apprehension. Two Bits stood about sixteen hands high and the ground looked too far away.

"He's a good horse," Nicholas assured her. "He'll be fine."

"Fine is good. Let's go then," she said, trying to project calm into her voice.

"Okay." Nicholas clucked to his horse and turned its head. "Let's go, Bud."

His horse gave a tiny jump, but then settled down and started a steady walk in the direction Trista and Lorne had gone.

Two Bits obediently followed Bud, his movement causing her to sway lightly in the saddle. Cara tried not to grab the pommel and forced herself to keep from squeezing Two Bits with her legs.

The saddle will keep you on, she reminded herself. *Just relax. You're not running a horse race.*

She took a few calming breaths. The warm summer air, the faint buzzing of insects and the regular footfalls of the horse's hooves on the packed ground lulled her into a sense of security.

She chanced a look ahead, watching Nicholas from behind.

Nicholas glanced sideways at the fields they rode beside, a smile curving his lips.

This is where he belongs, Cara thought, looking at him now silhouetted against the mountains. *This is his natural setting.*

Pain twisted Cara's heart.

And where do you belong?

Before she met Nicholas, the question had resonated through her life. Then, for those few, magical months with Nicholas she thought she had found her place.

And now?

Tomorrow will worry about itself. Each day has enough trouble of its own.

The passage from the Bible leaped into her mind, as if to underline her resolve. She was expending too much energy wondering how to react to Nicholas and thinking of how to behave around him.

They were outside on this beautiful day and were headed out into the hills. *Just enjoy it. Don't put extra burdens on it.*

Nicholas sat easily on his horse, his one hand on his thigh, the other loosely holding the reins. He had rolled his shirtsleeves up over his forearms, and as he rode, she could see his broad shoulders moving ever so slightly in response to the movement of the horse.

He's an extremely good-looking man, she thought with a touch of wistfulness.

And he doesn't belong to you anymore.

Chapter Seven

Cara and Nicholas reached the end of the field and turned on the trail where Trista and Lorne had gone moments before.

The trail started climbing almost immediately, winding through the dusky coolness of towering spruce and pine trees. In the light-strewn openings between the foliage, Cara caught glimpses of hayfields below them. The swaths Nicholas had cut were green and lush, thanks to recent rains. She knew, from talking to other farmers and ranchers, that this year would be productive.

"How much of this belongs to you and your father?" Cara asked, raising her voice so Nicholas could hear.

Nicholas glanced back and pushed his cowboy hat farther up on his head. "What you see below you is ours up to the river. Beyond that is Olsen's land." He pointed with one gloved hand.

Cara leaned to one side to see better, squinting a little until she saw the river.

"That's quite a lot of property."

"That's the hay land. We have pasture farther up the trail and we lease a bunch of land, as well."

Cara easily heard the pride in his voice as her eyes followed the contours of the land.

She knew, oh, how well she knew, how much this land meant to him. Hadn't he chosen this over her?

She tried to look at it through his eyes, to understand why she had been second choice.

The land was beautiful, the setting almost postcard perfect.

"Are your other cows up there?" she asked, thinking of the herd she saw close to the ranch.

"The purebred herd is in the pasture by the barn and the commercial herd is farther up," Nicholas explained. "I like to keep them separate as much as possible. And because I'm shipping heifers from the purebred herd, I wanted to keep them closer to the house so I could monitor their feed better."

"Did you buy this land or did it come with the ranch when your father took it over?"

Nicholas stopped his horse and Two Bits kept going until the two horses were side by side.

"My great-grandfather proved one quarter and

bought a few more from the neighbors who were struggling. He started there, by the river, using a horse and his own manpower." Nicholas pointed to a small peninsula of land. "My grandfather expanded on that using an old tractor and my dad used a bulldozer to clear it all the way up to the fence line you see."

She nodded, still looking at the land. For the first time since Nicholas chose the ranch over her, she got a tiny inkling of why this meant so much to him.

"My great-great-grandfather started with a small herd of cattle and a horse-drawn plow for the grain land, and it's been growing since. My grandfather thought he'd try exotics and dabbled in Charolais and Simmental, but my dad and I went back to Angus. And now I'm breaking into purebreds. And we've always grown grain and canola on the river-bottom lands."

Cara didn't imagine the note of pride in his voice as he spoke of the ranch and she envied him the history. Her grandmother was also a single mom and had moved around as much as her mother had. She had passed away before Cara moved in with Uncle Alan and Aunt Lori. She didn't know who her father was—her mother had told her repeatedly that he died working overseas and that was all she needed to know.

All she had was her uncle and aunt, a few faded

photographs and some stories that Uncle Alan would dredge up if pressed. Nicholas had a ranch steeped in history and generations of ancestors who were buried in a local churchyard.

"With each generation the ranch got a bit bigger," Nicholas said. "And with each generation it got easier to find a way to feed more cows and farm more land without hiring a whole bunch of people."

"And now it's just you and your dad."

"Yup."

She knew his history but because of Nicholas's work and because of his father's antagonism toward her, she'd caught only glimpses of the rest of the ranch. They had started dating in September, then Nicholas went away to work for a couple of months. When he came back, winter had arrived.

During his time off, their dates consisted of going out to movies, going out for coffee, some ski trips to Banff and visits with Uncle Alan and Aunt Lori. When Nicholas left again for work and returned with a broken leg, Cara thought he would quit.

But when the leg healed and spring came, he got a call for another job and took it.

As a result, she had never seen the ranch like this.

Would things have been different between them if she'd seen this earlier?

She pushed the question aside. What was done was done. Nicholas's choices were still difficult for her. That much hadn't changed.

"Did any of your ancestors ever think about moving somewhere else?" She knew the answer to this one, too, but she liked hearing him talk about his ranch. When he did, his voice softened and he became the Nicholas she remembered, the Nicholas she had fallen in love with.

"I've told you about Lily, my dad's sister who lives in Idaho," Nicholas said. "And my great-grandfather had a brother who moved back to England, but the rest of us stayed here."

"You told me once about your grandfather building a house somewhere else."

Nicholas stopped his horse and pointed through the trees to a small building tucked in some trees and edged with lilac bushes.

"Can you see that?" he asked. "That's it, right there."

"So why did he abandon it?" She knew his great-grandfather had moved the main residence to where it stood now, overlooking the valley.

"Too close to the river," he said. "They got drowned out once and my great-grandmother insisted on the move. She was a feisty one. I never knew her, but my grandfather and dad had a bunch of stories to tell about her."

"Like what?" Cara asked, intrigued by this unexpected chapter in the Chapman family history.

"I guess a porcupine was hanging around the yard one day chewing on some apple trees she had just planted. So she was going to get out the gun and kill it, but when she saw it looking at her, she couldn't. So she shot over its head to chase it away. Had to do that for the rest of the summer. She went through a lot of bullets chasing it away. Claimed she missed seeing it when it didn't show up one day." He smiled at the memory and Cara's heart hitched at the sight. Nicholas looked more relaxed than he had since she had come to Cochrane. The ranch agreed with him. It was where he belonged.

She shifted in the saddle, forcing her attention back to the land below them. "It's beautiful. I can see why it means so much to you."

Nicholas shot her a puzzled glance. "Can you?"

"It's been a part of your family for a long time."

Nicholas leaned on the pommel of his saddle, and as he looked out over the open fields, his voice tinged with pride. "We put a lot of ourselves into this place. When Mom left—" Nicholas stopped there.

As he often did.

Cara didn't know much about Nicholas's mother, Barb, only that she had suddenly left his father and Nicholas one day. Left a note on the table and a casserole in the oven.

"When your mom left," Cara prompted, wondering if she'd hear a bit more from him.

Nicholas sighed, his movement causing the saddle to creak. "Doesn't matter. That was a long time ago."

He straightened and it was as if a shutter dropped over his face. Cara experienced a glimmer of frustration. When they were dating she'd tried to get him to open up about his mother and his relationship with his father. But every time the conversation veered close to his parents, he shut down.

She had always assumed they would have time to find out more about each other. To encourage each other in their faith.

To grow together.

But that didn't happen.

"It's a terrible thing when a marriage falls apart," Nicholas said. "That's why I'm worried about Lorne and Trista."

Cara felt as if gears in her mind were grinding with the sudden shift in topic.

Obviously still not ready to talk about his mother and father's relationship, she thought. Or maybe Nicholas didn't think she warranted a glimpse into his private life.

"I'm concerned, too," she said, going along with the conversation, aware that Nicholas's concerns were hers. "Do you think he's getting cold feet?"

"I'm not sure." Nicholas tugged on the reins, turning his horse on another trail, leaving the open fields behind them. "I haven't had a chance to talk to him. I want to make sure Lorne doesn't go through the same thing I did."

Though he tossed the words out casually they wounded with precision.

"I think he and Trista are pretty committed to each other," Cara said quietly, trying to mask her own hurt as she kept her eyes on the landscape below them. "They've both made some sacrifices to make this relationship work, regardless of how it's starting out." She chanced a quick sideways glance and caught his frown. As if he didn't understand.

A relentless current of frustration washed through her. This lack of understanding of the sacrifices necessary for a relationship had dogged their own.

"At any rate, Trista seems nervous," Nicholas said.

"She doesn't do pressure well."

"None of us do."

It's just a casual comment, Cara reminded herself. *Don't read more into it than what's on the surface.*

But as their eyes connected, she caught a glimmer of an older, deeper emotion that made her wonder just how off-the-cuff this, and his previous comment, actually were.

"I know she loves Lorne and wants to marry him," Cara said, determined to keep this conversation on their friends. "But there's something else going on."

"We better figure out what it is before things go too far and I end up stuck with a bunch of guests and a caterer and no bride and groom."

"I doubt it will get that far," Cara said. "I think they've got a lot to deal with, but I have a feeling they'll find their way through this. I think they love each other enough."

Nicholas sighed heavily and his horse jumped a little to one side. He settled it down, then shot her a quick, sideways glance. "I guess that's always enough." His voice sounded wry.

Cara's heart began a slow, heavy beating and her face grew flushed. "What do you mean?" Cara said, wishing her voice didn't sound so strangled.

Nicholas slashed the air with his hand. "Nothing. Just slipped out."

Cara's hands clenched a little tighter on the reins. And then she felt a shiver of frustration. Until this wedding was done, they would be spending more time together.

It might make things easier for both of them if they confronted what had happened.

And how would that help? Nicholas had made it clear that their relationship was over.

But the few glances they had exchanged, the few moments of connection hovered in her mind. And she had missed that so badly when she left. Though she had gone on a few dates herself, she had never found the same rapport, the same connection she and Nicholas had shared.

She was leaving, so why not get some of this out of the way? What could it hurt?

"Do you think we didn't love each other enough?"

Cara wasn't aware she had voiced the question aloud until she saw Nicholas's head spin toward her.

"Why do you ask?"

"That came up in our last conversation," she said, keeping her attention on the trail winding ahead of them. She eased one foot out of the stirrup, thankful for the cramp in her foot to distract her.

"That wasn't a conversation, Cara. That was a conflagration."

Cara turned to him. "What else could I say? I asked for something from you that you couldn't give. Something I thought was important for our future relationship."

"Did you have any idea how much your request would cost me? Would cost the ranch?"

"Or would cost your father?"

Nicholas frowned. "What do you mean by that?"

Cara knew she had ventured into territory she had never dared set foot on when she and Nicholas were dating.

But that was when she thought she had something to lose. Now nothing was at stake except her own wounded pride and an inexplicable desire to have Nicholas see the situation from her viewpoint.

"I think it's easier for your father when you work so much."

Nicholas's frown warned her, but she had gone this far, she may as well keep going. She struggled to articulate her thoughts without sounding as if she didn't like his father.

She was about to speak when a coyote bolted across the trail.

Nicholas's horse startled, reared and bumped into Two Bits.

And everything went crazy.

Cara saw the world spin once as her horse twisted. She made a quick grab for the saddle horn, but missed.

She flew sideways and hit the ground with a bone-jarring crack. An electrical charge jolted up her head into her neck. Her vision went dark.

"Cara. Cara. Are you okay?"

Was that Nicholas sounding so angry? She blinked, trying to get her bearings, pushing herself up by her elbows. She heard a thumping of hooves and turned just as Nicholas's mount bolted back down the trail. Its stirrups flapped and its feet pounded out a mad rhythm in time to the thundering in Cara's chest.

Then Nicholas crouched at her side, his hands pushing her hair back from her face. "Are you okay?" he repeated, his fingers moving over her head, his arm supporting her shoulders.

She tried to move away but he held her down.

"Don't move. I want to make sure nothing's broken," he said, his voice firm.

She chanced a look up at his face, inches from hers, his eyes dark with concern.

"I'm okay," she said, feeling as if someone had robbed her breath.

"You don't sound okay," he said, his fingers grazing her temple, fingering through her hair.

It was his gentle touch and his arms around her that caused her voice to sound so strained. So unsure.

"Really, I'm fine." She struggled to her feet, swaying as she tried to regain her balance.

But he was there to catch her. She leaned against him, and once again let him hold her up.

Just until I get my balance, she promised herself, her hands resting lightly on the front of his shirt. *Just for the smallest moment,* she thought as her fingers curled against the warmth of his chest.

She closed her eyes, fighting the sudden wave of longing threatening to sweep her hard-won independence away.

She couldn't give in. Nothing had changed and she would only endanger her heart again.

And slowly, feeling as if she were pulling herself back from a dangerous precipice, Cara lowered her hands and drew back.

"Really, I'm fine," she said.

But Nicholas kept his hands on her arms.

"I want to get you back to the house."

"What about Lorne and Trista?" she asked.

"They'll figure things out soon enough." Nicholas's eyes flitted over her features. Then he frowned and brushed his fingers over a tender spot on her one temple. "I'm more worried about this bump."

Cara wanted to protest one more time, but then a wave of dizziness hit her and the concerned look on Nicholas face told her he saw it, too.

He whistled, Cara heard the sound of hoofbeats and then Two Bits came up beside Nicholas.

"Why did that other horse run away?" Cara asked, blinking hard to get her eyes into focus as Nicholas caught the reins. "Did you get bucked off?"

"No." Nicholas sounded insulted at her question. "I bailed when I saw you hit the dirt. And while I was distracted he reared and pulled the reins out of my hands."

Cara nodded, then wished she hadn't. The ache in her forehead was spreading.

"Here. You're going to ride," he said, looping Two Bit's reins over his head.

"I don't think so. I'll walk." She wasn't ready to get back on a horse again.

"It's too far and I don't want you falling over."

Cara was about to protest again when, in one smooth motion, Nicholas had her up on the saddle and then he was right behind her.

She felt as if she should put up some token resistance, but realized that was foolish. If she had a concussion, she couldn't walk, nor could she ride on her own. Nicholas was being practical.

But her pragmatic analysis couldn't explain away the increased tempo of her heart, and the tingle rushing to the tips of her fingers at his nearness.

"Relax," he murmured, slipping one arm around her waist and pulling her back. "You'll get a headache sitting all tense like that."

"I'm not tense." But in spite of her protestation, she had to force herself to rest against his chest.

His chin rubbed the side of her head and if she peeked up, she could see the brim of his hat and a piece of his hair hanging down over his face.

As if he sensed her attention, he angled his head downward. "Do you have a headache?"

"Just a bit." She forced her gaze ahead, watching the trail as the horse walked down it.

"Double vision?"

"So you're a doctor now?" she joked, trying to find equilibrium in humor when she was far too aware of the strength of his arm holding her close and the warmth of his chest against her back.

"I've taken a few spills. Had a concussion once."

"I don't think I have a concussion. I fell on the dirt."

He nodded and she didn't know what else to say.

So they rode in silence. Each second added to her mental and physical discomfort as the silvery beginnings of a headache made itself known and the nervous knot in her stomach tightened with each footfall from the horse.

"So how—"

"When do you—"

They both spoke at once, as if each were trying to pierce the same discomfort.

"Sorry—"

"Go ahead—"

Silence again.

"When do you have to bale the hay?" she asked, needing to talk about something.

"This week sometime, if the weather holds. We've got about one hundred and sixty acres to roll up and it's running pretty heavy, so that should keep me busy."

"Do you do it all up in round bales?"

Oh, listen to you, sounding all rancherlike.

She ignored the mocking inner voice. She was simply making conversation. Nothing more. Trying to sound interested in what Nicholas was interested in.

"I have an old square baler from my grandfather that I use to make up small square bales for the horses. The rest I do up in the large round bales."

"How many horses do you and your father have now?" Good job. She sounded much calmer.

"Ten. Dad sold four last year."

"Why?"

"So he could buy more horses."

Cara wasn't sure if she imagined the edge of frustration in his voice. "But you still have your dad's roping horse, Duke."

"Yeah. He'll be staying on the ranch until he's dead. Probably put him beside Jake, his brother. He died two years ago."

"Most people bury hamsters and goldfish out back," Cara joked.

His laughter rumbled up his chest as she stared at the trail ahead, a soft breeze teasing her hair. "Those we bury closer to the house," he said. "Don't take up as much space."

"You had hamsters?"

"A couple. I was better with big animals than small ones."

"I know the feeling. I don't care for working with smaller animals as much as horses and cows."

"So why do you work with small animals then?"

She felt caught on the barbs of her casual comment. "Well, it's easier to find a job in small animal care. And I can move around a bit easier."

"Which is important to you?"

She bit her lip, unsure of how to answer him and thankfully, he didn't follow up on the question.

They rode quietly for a while and his chest rose and fell, then again, as if he was about to ask her a question.

But nothing.

They were back to the beginning and she didn't want to return there. For a few wonderful moments, they had shared the easy rapport they had before their breakup and, despite her caution to herself, she was drawn again to this man.

You're moving on, she reminded herself.

Yes, but wouldn't it be easier if she left on better terms with Nicholas than she had the last time?

"When your great-great-grandfather came, was there much of a town?" she asked. She knew the best way to draw Nicholas out was to talk about the land beneath their feet.

Nicholas shifted in the saddle, the arm holding her close to him loosening a little, as if he had released some tension.

"Cochrane was just a small outpost when he came from England."

"That was about 1887?"

"Yeah." She sensed his puzzlement but pushed on.

"So did he come with a wife, or did he meet her here?"

"Actually, she was a mail-order bride."

"And how did that work out?"

"Good, I guess. Apparently she wasn't crazy about the ranch at first. She was from London, but she had chosen to come and made the best of it. Later the land drew her in and she grew to love it."

"Like I said, I can see why."

A heavy silence fell between them.

"Could you have?" he finally asked.

The question hung between them and Cara wasn't sure how to answer it.

"I guess we'll never know," was all she could say.

"I guess."

Did she imagine the wistful note in his voice? Did he miss her as she had missed him?

She took a chance and angled her head so she could see him better. And her heart hammered in her chest when she caught him looking down at her.

Their faces were mere inches apart. She could feel his breath, warm and gentle on her cheek.

The moment trembled between them and then,

slowly, Nicholas's head shifted, she turned her face and their lips brushed each other.

Cara closed her eyes, as Nicholas kissed her again, her hand coming up to cradle his jaw, then slipping up to touch his cheek.

Her breath left her as her emotions veered between doubt and longing, between yearning and common sense.

She wasn't staying here and neither was Nicholas. Yet…

She waited a moment. Just one more moment to treasure this kiss and store it away.

"Cara, what's happening?" he whispered.

And his quiet question jolted her back to reality.

What they had done was a dangerous and costly mistake. Once again things had altered between them but where could it go? Nothing in either of their lives had changed.

And yet, in this moment, it was as if the ground beneath her had shifted.

She pulled her scattered emotions together, withdrawing back into herself.

Thankfully they were out into the open and heading toward the corrals. The ride was coming to an end.

They arrived just as Nicholas's father pulled into the yard with his truck.

Cara caught the angry look on Dale's face

when he saw the two of them astride Two Bits. What would he have thought of the kiss she and Nicholas had shared?

What was she to think of it?

Chapter Eight

Nicholas helped Cara off the horse, and tried not to let his hands linger on her waist as she got her feet under her.

"You sure you're okay?" he asked. "I feel like we should take you to the hospital."

"I'm fine," she said.

"So, what's Bud doing, hanging around the corrals with the saddle still on?" Dale asked as he walked toward them. His narrowed eyes flicked from Cara to Nicholas as if looking for any hint of indiscretion.

Nicholas felt like a kid caught with his hand in the candy jar, then he dismissed the feeling. He was an adult. He'd held the woman he was once supposed to marry in his arms.

That he kissed her was simply a throwback to old, unresolved emotions.

Yeah, he could tell himself that but deep down

he knew better. He knew something had dramatically altered after that kiss. At least it had for him.

"Had a little spill up on the hills," Nicholas said, fighting down a beat of frustration at his father's unexpected arrival.

Usually his dad spent at least ten hours at the auction mart. He had counted on that when he and Cara went on their ride.

"The two of you went riding?" Dale asked.

"We were going with Lorne and Trista to check out a place to take pictures," Nicholas said. He turned to Cara. "I'm driving you home."

"I'm fine. Really," she protested. "No headache, no dizziness."

"But that bruise—"

Cara put her hand on his arm to stop him. "I'll get my aunt to bring me to the hospital if necessary. You should go get Lorne and Trista sorted out."

He saw the necessity of that. "You'll let me know if anything changes?"

"I will." She didn't look at him as she walked to her car and got in. Was she regretting their kiss?

Should he?

"You going to unsaddle Bud?" his father said.

Nicholas pulled his attention away from Cara.

"Why don't you do that?" he said. "I've got to take Two Bits back to find Lorne and Trista."

And before his father could ask him anything more about Cara, Nicholas was on his horse and gone. He had too much to think about. Too much to process.

And he wasn't about to do that in front of his father.

Fifteen minutes later he found Lorne and Trista heading back down the trail.

"Where's Cara?" Trista asked, as soon as she saw him.

"She had a spill and went home."

"You let her go on her own? You didn't bring her? What if she has a concussion?" Trista's questions hammered at him as they rode back to the ranch.

"She said she felt fine. She insisted on going on her own. What else could I do?" Nicholas said, his guilt making him testy. "You know how stubborn Cara can be."

"I suppose," Trista said with a sigh. "Did she talk to you about picking up plants from the nursery Tuesday?"

Nicholas glanced back at her. "No. What plants?"

"For the wedding. The nursery is having a closing-out sale, but she didn't think she would have enough room in her car to get them," Trista said. "I told her to ask you for help."

They'd had other things on their minds obviously.

"I don't know. I've got hay to bale and I have to move my cows to another pasture. The tractor needs an oil change and I've got to work on the corrals."

"I'll do the oil change tomorrow night," Lorne said. "And help you with the corrals. Your hay won't be ready to bale until Wednesday, which means you'll have time to help Cara with the plants."

"Why are you so eager to help?" He'd been getting a weird vibe from Lorne and Trista and harbored a faint suspicion they were playing matchmaker.

"Hello? Wedding? Here?" Lorne spread his hands out in an innocent gesture. "The more I can help you with, the more you can do."

So why didn't he go and get the plants? But he knew if he asked, he wouldn't get a straight answer.

"Okay, find out when she's going and I'll meet her there," he said.

Trista's grin gave him pause but he didn't want to speculate on what caused it. He had a faint suspicion that he knew what Trista was up to.

And the trouble was, he didn't mind.

* * *

"So as a friend, I need to ask. You absolutely certain Trista's the one for you?" Nicholas picked up the two-by-six, glancing across the pile of wood to his friend. He had been mulling over the questions he and Cara had discussed yesterday and knew he had to talk to his friend.

Lorne moved the piece of straw he'd been chewing on to the other side of his mouth and picked up the other end of the board. "Yeah. I am."

"And you two are happy together?" Nicholas set the board in place and braced it with his hip as he pulled his hammer out of the loop on his pouch.

"A lot happier than I was with Mandy and about as happy as you were with Cara."

Nicholas chose to ignore that last comment. Ever since the aborted ride yesterday, Lorne had been dropping hints about Cara as heavy as the board they were maneuvering into place.

"Just make sure you protect yourself," Nicholas muttered, pulling a handful of nails out of the pocket of his carpenter pouch. "You're starting a new business. If this marriage doesn't work—"

"I'm not going to lie, I have my concerns, as well, but Trista and I really love each other and we want to get married. And sometimes you just have to dive in. Take a chance. Love is a risk, but I think it's a risk worth taking."

"I took a chance with Cara. Getting engaged after seven months. Look where that got me." He easily pounded the nails in and Lorne followed suit.

"But you never set a wedding date, man."

Nicholas shrugged Lorne's comment aside. "That was only part of the problem."

Trouble was even though he had loved Cara, he had his own embers of misgivings. Misgivings fanned into flame by his father's concerns.

It wasn't part of the plan, his father had advised. Things needed to get done on the ranch first.

"Taking a chance can have serious repercussions," Nicholas said, walking back to get another board. "You're starting a business and you're not set up yet. Don't you think you should wait?"

"No. What Trista and I did was wrong and I want this baby born into a marriage."

"But you don't seem committed. You're letting Trista and Cara do most of the work."

"Hey, I'm committed to the marriage—the wedding is just what I have to do to get there. It's just a tradition."

"But it's a good one," Nicholas said as they carried the board back to the corrals.

"Says the guy who knows all about it," Lorne said as he grinned.

Nicholas ignored him. "If I was getting married I'd want things done proper and in order. Things need to be ready. In place."

"And that's why in a few days I'm getting married and you're still single."

"What do you mean?"

"You wanted everything just so before you and Cara got married. Bills paid, bank account solid, debt paid down. Corrals fixed, barn painted, all that jazz. But things get in the way and things happen and it can all be gone in a flash." Lorne snapped his fingers to underline his statement. "So maybe I'm taking a chance, but if you never take a chance, you never get to experience the thrill of jumping off into the void without a net." Lorne's voice held a touch of amusement.

"You, my friend, have been reading too many motivational books. Next thing I know you're going to tell me I need to release myself from the bonds of earth and fly free."

Lorne grew quiet and for a moment Nicholas thought he might have hit a nerve.

Nicholas glanced up in time to see his friend looking at him with a steady gaze, his hammer hanging at his side.

"What?" Nicholas asked.

"You go to church, dude. You know that God wants us to do justice, to love mercy and to walk humbly with Him—at least that's how I remember it. I'm taking care of my responsibilities so I'm doin' that. I know you don't wanna talk about Cara, but you made a megamistake with her. And I figure you got a second chance, now that she's back."

"She's got her own plans, Lorne. And they don't include me."

Lorne gave no reply and for a while the only noise that broke the quiet was the ringing of hammers and the occasional bellow from the herd of heifers close to the barn.

But as they worked Lorne's words as well as his confidence in what he was doing spun around Nicholas's mind.

"Oh, brother. What's this doing on here?" Lorne brushed some sparrow droppings off the boards. "Those birds are getting to be a pest. You really need to do something about 'em."

"And a million other things," Nicholas said. "I can't keep up."

"Have you ever thought of quitting your job?"

"You sound like Cara used to," Nicholas muttered.

"So what happened with you and Cara?" Lorne asked.

Nicholas missed the nail he was hammering and bent it over. "Nothing. We just had a spill.

She fell and then Bud took off. So I thought I should bring her back. So, nothing happened."

Lorne snickered and Nicholas straightened the nail. "I was talking about how you two broke up, dude."

"I...I told you," he said, wishing he didn't sound so flustered. "We had a fight about my job."

"So I'm guessing something else happened between you and Cara on Sunday," Lorne asked, his voice full of innuendo.

Nicholas pounded the nail home in three swipes. He had never been a kiss-and-tell kind of guy and wasn't spilling his guts to a friend in wedding mode. "She had a spill. Nothing else happened."

"Else?"

He clamped his lips together. Best not to say anything more.

But as he fitted another nail in the board, his mind slipped back to that fateful kiss. He wished he could rewind that moment. He should never, never have done that. It was a mistake and he had to make sure he got through this wedding with his heart whole.

Chapter Nine

"And I'll take two dozen of these gerberas," Cara said to the greenhouse attendant, leaning over the wooden table to point out the one she wanted.

The swish of the sprinklers, the abundant greenery and the humid warmth of the greenhouse created a sense of wonder and expectation in Cara.

She wished she had her own place, a garden and flower beds. She let her mind wander to Nicholas's house, imagining plants nestled against the wooden step leading up to the house and flowers hanging from the porch. The place looked immaculate, but it needed a woman's touch. Some flowers, some shrubs. A kitchen garden—

"And you wanted a dozen of the pre-poted arrangements?" the clerk asked, his question breaking into her runaway and foolish thoughts.

She tapped her finger on her chin, considering. "Actually, make that fifteen."

She did some mental calculations, figuring what plants she would need where, and then her phone rang. She glanced at the call display. Trista.

"Hey, Cara, are you at the nursery already?" she demanded.

"I got off work early."

"Okay. Okay, that should work. Let me think."

Cara frowned as she pinched a dead flower off one of the plants. "What should work?"

"I got Nicholas to meet you at the nursery. I thought we should bring the plants to the ranch right away. That way they don't have to get moved twice."

Cara swallowed against the anticipation that filled her at the sound of Nicholas's name. She didn't want to see him so soon. Not after Sunday.

Of its own accord her hand drifted up to her mouth. It was as if his kiss still lingered on her lips. His touch still warmed her.

"That won't work," she protested. "Who is going to water them?"

"Nicholas said he didn't mind."

A picture of Nicholas wielding a watering can flashed into Cara's mind. "He doesn't have time. Any day now he's baling his hay."

"And you know that...how?"

Cara chose to ignore the innuendo in Trista's voice. "When is Nicholas coming?"

"He should be there in about five minutes. He's taking his flatbed truck so you should be able to put all the plants on it. I gotta run. Thanks a ton for doing this." And then Trista broke the connection.

Cara put her phone away, disappointed to see her hands trembling. Nicholas was coming.

She had hoped to avoid him for a few more days. At least until her heart didn't do that silly pounding thing every time she thought of him. At least until her emotions could settle down.

She'd just have to speed up the process.

She was paying for the plants when, in the edge of her vision, she caught a shadow in the doorway of the nursery. The fine hairs on her arm rose up, her neck grew warm and she knew, without looking up, that Nicholas stood there.

"Do you need help with these?" the clerk asked as he handed over her change.

"I'll help her." Nicholas now stood beside her, his presence filling the room.

She glanced up at him, disconcerted to see him looking down at her. A slow smile teased the mouth that had kissed her yesterday and as their eyes met, a shiver spiraled up her back.

"How's the injury?" he asked, a callused finger lightly touching the bruise on her forehead.

"The doctor said everything was fine." She forced her gaze away, forced her emotions under control.

"Do all of these need to come out?" Nicholas asked, gesturing at the plants.

"Every single one," she said.

Nicholas grabbed the handles of four plants and headed out the door, Cara holding only two plants, right behind him. Thankfully he had parked his truck right out the door.

"Why don't you stay here," he said, placing his plants on the truck bed, "and I'll bring the plants up to you."

"Sounds like a good idea." She was about to put her foot on the tire and climb up, when he grabbed her by the waist and hoisted her up.

She caught her balance, then turned away from him, busying herself with arranging the plants on the truck bed. This was ridiculous, she told herself. *Get a grip, woman.*

When he came out again, her control had returned and a few minutes later, all the plants were set out on the truck, ready to be moved.

"I'm glad I came," Nicholas said, glancing over the assortment of greenery and flowers. "It would have taken you forever to move these on your own."

"I could have managed," Cara said, trying mightily to create some emotional distance from the man looking up at her. "But, yeah, it's nice to have the help."

She made her way through the plants to the back of the truck determined, this time, to get down on her own.

"So do you want to follow me?" Nicholas asked when she was on the ground again.

Cara wanted to say no. She wanted to tell Nicholas to unload the plants himself and leave her alone. She didn't want to fall into the feelings swirling around her. Feelings that had the potential to overwhelm her and make her lose her footing once again.

And yet...

She looked up into his gray eyes and, for a moment, felt peace.

"I'll follow you," she said.

While she drove behind Nicholas's truck she phoned Aunt Lori to tell her she wasn't coming home for dinner. She assured her aunt that she would grab a bite to eat in town.

Twenty minutes later she pulled up behind Nicholas's truck. He was already taking the plants off the bed.

"I thought we could put them here," he said,

pointing with his chin to the porch. He hung up one pot, the pink petunias and blue trailing lobelia creating a bright spot of color and friendly welcome.

Her heart did a slow flip as he hung the second pot on another old hook beside the first one. The house now looked like a home.

She shook aside the feeling. She was here to work, not daydream.

In no time, plants hung from every available hook and were placed along the foundation of the house, brightening the drab wood siding and filling the empty flower beds.

"Hey, that looks great," Nicholas said, brushing the dirt off his hands, grinning at the brightly colored plants. "I might have to get into gardening next year. Spruce the place up."

"You'll have to water them regularly," Cara reminded him.

He shot her a quick smile. "I irrigate one hundred and sixty acres of hay. I think I can remember to do a few plants."

"Just saying, is all," Cara said, sharing his smile.

He stood, his hands on his hips, glancing from the plants to her as if not sure what to say next. "Trista asked if we could make a bit of a plan—figure out what you wanted where."

Cara glanced over toward the site. From here

she could see the arbor already in place and a sense of sorrowful déjà vu drifted over her. This was exactly how she had imagined her own wedding site.

"Did Mr. Elderveld put hooks in the top bar of the arbor?" Cara asked as they walked toward the site. "We'll need them to hang plants." Cara did a slow turn, thinking out loud. "I'd like to create some groupings of flowers of different heights, but I'm not sure what we can use."

"I have an old cream separator and a couple of cream cans we could put plants in," Nicholas suggested.

"Sounds great. Why don't you get them and we can figure out where to put them."

While he was gone, Cara put stakes in the ground where she wanted plant pots situated.

She heard the putt-putt of a small engine and turned, wondering what was going on.

Nicholas pulled up beside her, astride a green ATV, pulling a trailer. "I found two old wagon wheels, as well," he said, looking very proud of himself. "Thought we could use them somewhere."

Cara walked over to the trailer, her mind spinning with the possibilities. "Where did this come from?" she asked, running her hand over the antique machine. She didn't know how a cream separator worked. She did know that the large metal bowl on the top of the column would be a perfect holder for another plant. She bent over and read the plate. "Renfrew Machinery Company. 1924."

"My grandfather and great-grandfather milked cows." Nicholas gestured toward the red hip-roof barn. "My first memory of my grandmother was watching her clipping a cheesecloth on the basin and pouring milk from the cows into the separator. The skim milk would come out here, and the cream out here," Nicholas said, pointing to two spouts offset from each other. "Then she'd haul two five-gallon pails of milk off to the pigs." Nicholas smiled as he ran his hands over the machine. "She was a pretty tough woman, my grandmother."

"And your grandparents live in an old-age home now? In Calgary?"

"You remember?" Nicholas shot her a puzzled frown.

"I remember you talking about visiting them, yes." It hurt that he thought she had brushed away every conversation they'd ever had.

"I still go see them whenever I can."

"But no milk cows now?" Cara asked, trying to imagine Nicholas as a young boy watching his grandmother working on the same place he still lived. Cara had met her grandmother only once as she and her mother crisscrossed the continent.

Her grandfather had died before Cara was born and Cara's grandmother passed away fifteen years ago, but Cara hadn't grieved the death of a woman she barely knew.

"My dad got rid of the cows as soon as he took over the place. Gramps wasn't fond of them so he didn't mind. He just kept them around for Gramma's sake. They never made a lot of money off them. The real money was in cattle and grain." Nicholas brushed some dust off the large silver bowl mounted on the top, a melancholy smile edging his mouth.

"And working away from the farm." No sooner had the words slipped out than Cara felt like smacking her head.

Silence followed that and Cara turned her attention back to the job at hand.

"So, let's decide what we should put where," she said. "I think we could put the cream separator by the guest-book table and put one of the plants with the trailing lobelia in it."

"And the guest table is where?"

Cara walked to the spot and pushed a stake in the ground. Nicholas followed her with the ATV and hauled the separator out of the trailer.

"Next, we'll figure out where we want the chairs."

As they paced out, measured and planned, Cara drew on the plans she had made for herself for the brief months of her own engagement to Nicholas. She'd had it all figured out, down to where the guest book would be located and what would have been on the table.

"This is going to look great," Nicholas said, looking over the site.

"So, do you think this will all go through?" Cara asked, thinking of the dozens of cupcakes in her aunt's freezer. She and Trista had decided to forego the usual wedding cake in favor of a cupcake tower.

"Yeah. I really do."

Cara shot a quick glance Nicholas's way. "Did you talk to Lorne?"

"He's committed to her and to being married. I think his biggest problem was the hoopla surrounding the ceremony."

"I can understand. Most guys don't like the planning part of weddings." But even as she spoke, she thought of all the work Nicholas put into this wedding.

He was meticulous and he liked things done in good order. All part of his personality and one of the reasons they were standing here, planning someone else's wedding instead of their own.

Don't go there. Don't go there.

"I feel like things are coming together," Nicholas said, slapping some dirt off his blue jeans.

"You seem to know exactly what to do. How did you figure it all out?"

Cara crossed her arms, looking around the still-empty yard, seeing it the way she thought it would look when done. "I used the plans that I…" Her voice faded on the summer breeze sifting over the yard.

"Plans that you what?"

She shrugged, then figured she had nothing to lose and completed her sentence. "That I had in mind for…our wedding."

He said nothing and she didn't want to turn to catch his reaction. She didn't want to know if she'd see relief on his face because her plans never reached fruition, or if she'd see regret.

"You had actually thought that far?"

"I'm like any other girl," she said. "I made plans. Even bought a bride magazine."

She thought of their shared kiss, the tender way he had held her, and her heart stuttered with a mixture of pain and regret.

Should she have been so insistent on his staying away from his work?

But now, after seeing his love for the ranch, she knew more than before he would never put her needs before the needs of the place he loved so much.

"At least I get to use the plans now," she added, fighting a surprising wave of sorrow.

Then, to her alarm, Nicholas came to stand in front of her and his finger brushed over the bruise on her forehead.

"So how come we didn't get that far?" he asked.

Cara avoided his gaze. If she let herself be beguiled by him, she'd be headed down the same path they'd traveled before and she knew where that would end.

Nicholas would leave and she'd be left behind, afraid and worried.

So her and Nicholas? Dead end.

"Maybe we weren't meant for each other," she said quietly. "Maybe it wasn't meant to be."

"That sounds pretty vague to me."

Cara shrugged. "Maybe vague is all I can give you." She looked up at him then, taking a chance. "Maybe I can't give you any more than I already did."

Nicholas's eyes narrowed and for a moment she wondered if he understood what she meant.

"You left," he said, anger threading his voice. "You took off without a word. I thought you didn't want to marry me and now I find out that you were actually planning our wedding. So it wasn't the proposal that sent you scurrying away?"

Cara hardly dared to look at him, not sure he would fully understand. "No. It was your work. Your job."

Nicholas took a step back. "So we're still back to that?" He released a humorless laugh. "Back to where we started."

"Has anything changed?" she asked.

He opened his mouth, as if to speak, but she didn't want to hear it. Didn't want to hear him say that yes, he had to leave. Had to go work his dangerous job. Had to put the ranch ahead of everything.

"We're done here," Cara said, managing to keep her voice even as it broke into the awkward stillness drifting into the moment. Then she walked toward her car, quickening her pace, before the tears filling her eyes spilled over.

Chapter Ten

Cara sat cross-legged on her bed, her Bible on her lap flipping idly through it when she heard a knock on the door.

"Come in," she said, looking up from the book, but not closing it.

Her uncle put his head in the room. "I saw your light on. Everything okay?"

"Yeah. I'm okay." She gestured for him to come in and he grabbed a chair, carried it closer to her bed, sat down and caught his breath.

Though he claimed he was fine, Cara knew his recuperation was taking longer than he hoped.

"How was your day?" he asked. "I was napping when you got home."

"Long. Tiring." But not all her exhaustion had to do with the vet work she'd done today. Her thoughts kept edging toward the conversation she and Nicholas had on Tuesday then circling back to their time together on Sunday.

And every time she had to pull herself back to the present she felt a tiny sense of loss.

"I spent an hour with Anderson's mare, trying to deliver a colt and then spent three hours taking it apart so I could remove the body."

Uncle Alan patted her hand in commiseration. "Surgeries like that are disheartening and draining."

"I know. And that poor mare kept straining." Cara's voice hitched.

"At least you won't be doing that kind of work in Montreal," Uncle Alan said.

"No. Thank goodness." Cara tried to inject a note of relief into her voice, but in the past two weeks she'd been happier at work than she'd been for the past three years.

As to what that meant for her job in Montreal, she didn't want to ponder.

Uncle Alan gestured toward the Bible. "So, you started reading that again?"

Cara looked down at the book. She'd received it from her aunt and uncle when she graduated from high school. She had read it once in a while, but after her mother's death, she had put it away.

"I don't know if it's going to help," Cara said. "But lately I feel like I'm stumbling around in the dark—"

"God's word is a lamp unto my feet and a light unto my path." Uncle Alan gave her a gentle smile.

Cara laughed lightly. "Yeah, I guess I'm at the right place then."

"What are you reading?"

"I'm just paging through the Psalms."

"What are you looking for?"

Cara sighed as she flipped another page. "Guidance. Direction." She ran her fingers lightly down the page, as if trying to read the words by touch. "I don't know what's happening in my life anymore, Uncle. I have a plan. I know what I'm going to do and yet feel…lost."

"Are you talking about your job in Montreal?"

"It's a good job, Uncle Alan. I'll be able to do some traveling and I'll be challenged and there's lots of room for upward movement and career advancement." But as she spoke, Cara kept her eyes on her finger, still tracking the words in the Bible.

"Who are you trying harder to convince? Me or you?" he asked gently, leaning back in the chair, the light from her bedside lamp reflecting off his glasses.

Cara looked down at the Bible again and laughed. "I don't know. Both, I guess."

Uncle Alan heaved a heavy sigh. "If that

Gordon fellow wasn't coming I could give you a job here—"

"I don't want a job here." The words fairly jumped out of her.

"I hope you're not so adamant because you don't want to be working with me," Uncle Alan joked.

Cara riffled the pages of the Bible with one hand. "Of course not. I would love to work with you."

"So then I'm guessing it's Nicholas?"

Cara's head snapped up. Uncle Alan just smiled.

"I may be recuperating from a heart attack, but I'm not blind."

"I never thought you were."

"Be careful, Cara," he said. "Don't let your past feelings interfere with your current situation."

"You don't have to worry," Cara said. "In fact as soon as his cattle are tested he's going on an overseas job. Something more hazardous than the offshore rig work he used to do." Her voice caught, the emotions and weariness of the day piling on her.

Thankfully Uncle Alan didn't say anything. Instead he reached over and gently took the Bible from her unresisting hands. He angled his head up so he could see through his bifocals, licked his finger and turned a few pages. Then he handed the Bible back to her.

"Read this, my dear. Psalm 139 up to verse 18. Maybe that will give you some comfort."

Then he got up, bent over, brushed a kiss over her forehead and left.

As the door closed softly behind him, Cara swiped at the lone tear trickling down her cheek, blinked the rest away and bent her head to read.

"'Oh, Lord, You have searched me and know me,'" she read, "'You know when I sit and when I rise. You perceive my thoughts from afar.'" Cara stopped there, her mind ticking back to a time when the idea that God knew her thoughts frightened her. But now she realized God now knew her confusion.

And her fear.

She read on, letting the poetry of the words nourish and seep into her soul. "'Where can I go from Your Spirit? Where can I flee from Your presence? If I go up to the heavens, You are there; if I make my bed in the depths, You are there.'"

As she read, it was as if hands rested on her shoulders, easing away the burden she carried there.

She thought of what her aunt had told her, that

though she may have turned her back on God, He was still there. Still waiting.

Deep in her soul, she had always known that.

She closed her eyes and let her heart rest in God and rest in His love.

He had to be enough for her, she realized. She had to stop thinking she needed more than God.

"Forgive me, Lord," she prayed. "Help me not to look for happiness and contentment in other people. Help me to only seek You first."

And as she slowly released her hold on her plans, her life and her heart, peace stole over her soul.

And slowly she struggled to release her changing feelings for Nicholas into God's care.

Chapter Eleven

"Are you okay?" Trista held Cara by the shoulders, staring into her eyes.

Cara adjusted the gauzy veil on Trista's head and frowned. "Why are you asking me? Today is your wedding day." She knelt and fluffed up the dress, then stood back to admire her friend.

Yesterday she was wound as tight as a spring, making last-minute calls to the caterer, to Nicholas, to the minister, to Trista's mother. But it had all come together.

"I just want to make sure you're okay with Nicholas and all that."

"I'm fine. Trust me." And just to underline her statement, Cara gave Trista a bright smile, then turned her to face the mirror. "Look at you. You look amazing."

Trista's dress had been worn by her mother and altered to fit. The style was simple, but elegant.

Raw silk gathered on one hip by a jeweled pin, then fell in rich folds to the ground. The veil belonged to Lorne's mother. Just a simple layer of gauzy netting and a bandeau covered with a remnant of silk taken from the dress.

Cara looked over her friend's shoulder, smiling at their shared reflections—her blond hair pinned back on one side with a single flower, Trista's dark hair surrounded by a halo of white. "Remember the wedding plans we used to make?" she whispered, as if unwilling to disturb the moment.

"You always knew what you wanted," Trista said, reaching behind her for Cara's hand. "And just for the record, this should be you. You used to talk about getting married way more than me."

"Just silly games," Cara said, trying to laugh off Trista's concern. Dredging up old dreams and memories was a waste of time.

Trista turned and caught Cara's other hand and gave them a light shake. "I still believe you'll find the right person."

"Thanks, Trista, but today is your day." Cara adjusted her veil and wiped away a tiny smudge of mascara from her cheek. "And we're not discussing me anymore." She glanced around the room, looking for the bouquet.

Nicholas had cleared out an empty bedroom in the house for Trista's changing room and had found an old, full-length mirror. Probably an antique, Cara guessed, from the aged wood framing it. Probably something his great-grandmother used.

Trista ran her hands down the raw silk of her dress and placed her hands on her stomach. "I don't show yet, do I?"

"Not even the tiniest bump," Cara assured her.

She saw a florist's box on the bed and pulled out Trista's bouquet. The bouquet was made of white roses offset with blue larkspur tied loosely together with a blue silk ribbon matching the blue silk of Cara's dress.

Cara's bouquet was made up of blue larkspur.

"So you go first, then I do, right?" Trista asked with a grin. "Or is it the other way around?"

"I told you we should have had a rehearsal," Cara said.

"As Lorne says, what's to rehearse?" Trista leaned closer to the mirror and dabbed at her lipstick. "We're not doing anything fancy." She pressed her lips together then inhaled deeply, her hand on her stomach. "Besides, there wasn't time. Lorne and I barely got the marriage classes done."

"We've been to enough weddings. I'm sure we'll figure it all out," Cara said, though on one level, she was thankful there hadn't been a rehearsal either. Spending an evening with Nicholas at a wedding that had been based on her own plans was difficult enough. Two nights in a row would have been too hard.

You've got a good job waiting, she told herself. *A job that will finance any trip you might want to make. You can go anywhere and do anything.*

Just like your mother did.

Cara ignored the mocking voice. Her mother had a child that she left behind. She was leaving no one behind in her life. No hearts would break when she left.

And after she had spoken to Uncle Alan, she had drawn more comfort from the Bible. God would not leave her and that was enough for her.

A knock at the door made them both jump. "Are we ready?" As Trista's father came into the room, he shook his head in amazement.

"My girl," he said, with a little hitch in his voice. "You look so beautiful." He embraced his daughter and Cara caught the shimmer of tears in his eyes.

And she would be lying if she said she wasn't jealous.

She had Uncle Alan and Aunt Lori and she was thankful she still had both in her life. If she were to get married, he would walk her down the aisle.

Yet that didn't seem the same as a father who had raised her from a baby, who had seen every step of her growth, looking with pride at his own daughter on this momentous day.

Trista's father pulled back and he shook his head, as if he couldn't understand himself how the years had slipped away.

"I'm so proud of you, honey," he said. "You've been a blessing to me and your mother and I pray you will be a blessing to Lorne."

Trista wiped a tear and Cara's throat thickened at this precious moment.

"Now, let's deliver you to your future husband." Mr. Elderveld patted her shoulder and gave her a bright smile.

They walked together down the stairs of Nicholas's house and down the wooden steps of the verandah. Ahead of them were the rows of chairs where the guests were seated. Pots of flowers lined the grass aisle, flanked the arbor and hung from the crosspiece, creating a riot of color set against the stunning backdrop of the mountains.

Soft music played from hidden speakers, adding to the ambience.

And as they approached, Cara saw the minister, Lorne and Nicholas already waiting.

Nicholas wore a navy suit and light blue shirt, echoing the colors of Cara's simple sheath. The shirt softened the gray of his eyes, giving them an azure tint.

The music changed, and Cara walked slowly toward the front. She kept her focus on the people in the audience smiling their encouragement as she walked past. She saw her aunt and uncle sitting in the crowd. Uncle Alan gave her a wink and Aunt Lori just smiled.

Then as she came to the front and took her place on the other side of the pastor, she chanced another quick look toward Nicholas.

This time he looked directly at her. His features were impassive and she wondered what was going on behind those gray-blue eyes of his that shifted away so quickly.

And why did that bother her?

Then the music changed to a solemn wedding march, everyone stood and Cara forced her gaze back to Trista. The gauzy veil framed her serene face and her white dress shimmered in the afternoon sun.

The smile on Trista's face transformed her and joy for her friend rippled through Cara. She looked so peacefully happy that Cara couldn't stifle another small jolt of jealousy.

That could have been me and Nicholas.

Cara gave Trista an encouraging smile and

then Trista had eyes only for Lorne. Lorne met Mr. Elderveld, then took Trista's hand and led her to the arbor.

A soft breeze and the faint buzzing of bees sifted through the air as the pastor looked around the gathering as if to underscore the solemnity of the occasion.

Then he faced Lorne and Trista.

"Dearly beloved, we are gathered here to celebrate the marriage of Lorne Hughes and Trista Elderveld. That we are all gathered as friends and family is important…"

It had all come together, Cara thought as the pastor spoke, her eyes ticking over the plants hanging from the arbor, nestled against the sides and hanging from hooks down the aisle. Though she hadn't been here to supervise, everything looked exactly as she had planned.

After that emotional moment with Nicholas, she had stayed away from the ranch, preferring to give instructions via Lorne and get updates via Trista. While she and her aunt decorated cupcakes and helped make table runners from the safety of her aunt's home, Cara heard the lawn on the yard had been mowed and the arbor set up.

An excited phone call from Trista had told her the wedding dress was finished and the bridesmaid dress had arrived at the store in Calgary.

She had heard that Nicholas rented a tent and got the chairs from the church. Nicholas was taking good care of the plants. The hay was baled but Nicholas was still crabby.

Yesterday Cara had told Lorne's brother how she wanted the chairs arranged and where she wanted the hooks and which plants to hang on them.

She'd immersed herself in her work and wedding plans and, with a lot of self-discipline and prayer, had managed to keep thoughts of Nicholas at bay.

Now, the day had arrived and things were moving along just as she had envisioned.

Just as she had planned for her own wedding.

She caught her thoughts from veering back down that treacherous path. Looking ahead was the only way she would survive this wedding. She had her own future to plan.

And who is in that future?

She pushed the insidious question aside. She was going it alone. It seemed to have worked for her mother, so she would make it work for herself.

Then, unable to stop herself, she glanced past Lorne to where Nicholas stood silhouetted against the valley of his ranch. Behind him lay green fields dotted with round, fat bales and, past that, the pastures and cropland of the Chapman ranch.

Nicholas had continuity and history.

He had his great-grandparents' cream separator that had been used on this place. He lived in the same home where he'd grown up.

He had roots and stability.

And she?

Since she broke up with Nicholas, the restlessness that had gripped her when her mother died had grown. She had tried to satisfy that by moving around. A restlessness, if she were to be honest with herself, still coursed through her.

But worse, she had been gripped with a loneliness that had claws.

"'Be content with what you have, because God has said, never will I leave you, never will I forsake you,'" the pastor was saying. "Trista and Lorne chose these words from Hebrews as a reminder to us of where true love comes from. A God who lavishes rich love on us."

The words caught Cara's attention.

Never will I leave you. Never will I forsake you.

And behind those words came the ones she had read the other night.

If I rise on the wings of the dawn, if I settle on the far side of the sea, even there Your hand will guide me, Your right hand will hold me fast.

The strength she'd received from those words returned to her. Strength and the reminder that though she had turned her back on God, as her Aunt Lori had said, God had not turned His back on her. It was as if, in her weak and weary moments, God was trying to catch her attention. To show her that though she may forsake Him, He hadn't forsaken her.

"...so this love that God lavishes on us is how we, too, should live our lives and live our marriages. God is a God of abundance and rich blessings if we acknowledge that He wants to walk alongside us and surround us in our marriages... and in our lives."

He paused to give the words their due and Cara felt a stirring of the same emotion that had touched her when she'd read the Bible the other night.

God alongside me, she thought, the gentle touch of His presence surrounding her.

Trista turned to her, handing Cara her bouquet, and then they were moving on to the next part of the ceremony. As Trista and Lorne exchanged their vows and then their rings, Cara felt a gentle melancholy. Her friend now belonged to someone else.

They exchanged a kiss and walked over to the table to sign the register. Cara clutched Trista's bouquet and her own and fell into step beside Nicholas. She tried not to be aware of his presence, tried not to feel overwhelmed by his nearness.

She placed the bouquets on the table. When she returned to Nicholas's side, she stepped into a depression in the grass and faltered in her high heels, but Nicholas caught her elbow and steadied her. His hand felt warm, callused. The hand of a man who worked.

And his touch sent a shock up her arm.

"Sorry about that," he murmured. "I didn't manage to get everything smooth."

She nodded her reply, focusing her attention on Trista sitting at the table.

When it was her turn to sign, she had to walk past Nicholas and she prayed she would keep her feet under her. As she sat down, she could feel him standing behind her.

Just help me get through this, she prayed, signing her name where the pastor showed her, pleased that her hands didn't tremble as much as her stomach did.

Then the pastor presented the new couple to the gathering and with a burst of joyous music, Lorne and Trista rushed down the aisle, as if eager to start their married life.

Nicholas held out his arm to Cara and she hesitated.

"We're supposed to do this," he said, sounding put out.

She was being silly. This was simply tradition. She slipped her arm in his and they followed the bridal couple down the aisle.

But as soon as they got to the end, he released her and walked away.

Her own reaction to him frustrated her. *Why do you have to be so touchy around him?* she scolded herself. *Why can't you act like he's some ordinary guy?*

Because he wasn't and never would be an ordinary guy to her. And in spite of the comfort she'd just received, she also knew, without a doubt, neither would Nicholas be the constant in her life that God would.

Thankfully there wasn't a receiving line so Cara didn't need to stand beside Nicholas, like some pretend couple, and receive well-wishers on her friend's wedding. Instead, people simply milled about, grabbing the opportunity to congratulate Lorne and Trista when they could.

Someone tapped her shoulder and Cara turned to see the photographer standing behind her.

In all the busyness, she had forgotten about him, she realized with a start. Trista didn't want pictures taken before the ceremony nor during and had simply told him to show up after the service.

"So, where are the horses we'll be taking into the mountains?" the photographer asked. "I might need an extra one for the equipment."

Cara's heart downshifted. She didn't want to get on a horse and ride up into the hills. Whenever she brushed her hair and touched the tender spot on her temple, she was reminded of her spill.

"Trista and I decided we're not going that route." Nicholas's deep voice spoke up from behind her. "We'll just take pictures on the yard."

Relief made her bones weak and she shot a grateful look his way, but he didn't catch her gaze.

"Could you get Lorne and Trista and meet us on the south side of the barn in about fifteen minutes?" he asked, then turned and strode away, the photographer trotting along behind just to keep up.

"I'll show you where you can set up," Nicholas called over his shoulder.

Cara felt a hand on her shoulder. "Oh, my dear, you look so beautiful." Aunt Lori gave her a tight hug, then brushed a strand of hair back from her face.

Uncle Alan hugged her next, but caught a glimmer of sympathy in his expression.

"You doing okay?" he asked, lowering his voice.

She gave him a bright smile. "I'm fine. I'm so happy for Trista."

Aunt Lori tapped him on the shoulder. "I think we should go now."

Cara frowned. "You're not staying for dinner?"

Aunt Lori glanced from Cara to Uncle Alan, as if unsure of what to say. "Alan's feeling a bit tired."

"I'm not that tired," he protested. "Just a bit…"

"Tired," Aunt Lori said firmly. She gave Cara a smile, then took Alan's arm. "You enjoy the rest of the evening. I won't be waiting up for you, though."

"Probably a good idea. I'll need to stay here until the end."

"Then we'll see you in the morning." And Aunt Lori turned, her arm in Uncle Alan's as they walked away, their steps measured and slow.

They were getting old. She was the only child they had and she was leaving them alone again. But she couldn't take that burden on. She had her own stuff to deal with.

At least they have each other, she thought, lifting up her dress and heading out to find the bride and groom.

A few minutes later she herded Trista and Lorne past well-wishers and fielded questions about the supper from Lorne and Trista's family as they went to meet the photographer.

By the time she got them to the barn, he was already set up and Nicholas looked as if he was about to come and get them.

"Finally," he said, frowning at everyone. "We've got to get this show on the road. We're already running about ten minutes behind."

Trista sent Cara a look of mock horror. "Oh, no. Ten whole minutes. Whatever shall we do?"

Cara laughed, but then caught herself when Nicholas sent her a grumpy look.

"The photographer wants to start with a group shot," Nicholas was saying. "Then he can focus on you and Lorne so Cara and I can get back to—"

"Bossing people around," Trista retorted. "Okay. Group shot. I don't want the usual standing in a row shot. I want me and Lorne together and Nicholas and Cara together."

They obediently arranged themselves as couples and the photographer fussed and adjusted with Lorne and Trista, then turned his attention to Cara and Nicholas.

"Put your hand here," he said to Nicholas, taking his hand and placing it on Cara's hip.

"We're not the bride and groom," Nicholas grumbled even as he did as he was told.

Cara swallowed as his hand dropped on her hip. This was just a show. Meant nothing at all.

"I just want to balance the shot," the photographer said, squinting at Cara, as if he wasn't sure what to do with her. "Could you move back toward Nicholas?"

She could, but she didn't want to. Already she felt too aware of Nicholas standing behind her, the warmth of his chest, the scent of his cologne. But she obediently took a small step backward.

"Good. That's better. Now if you could look down at your bouquet, hold it up a bit more, and, Nicholas, could you put your hand over hers? That's great."

Cara jumped a bit as Nicholas's fingers covered her hand. They were like ice.

She chanced a quick look up at him and their gazes met.

Just for a moment she caught a flare of another emotion in his eyes. The same emotion she'd seen moments before he'd kissed her the other day.

But he blinked and she wondered if she had imagined it.

She jerked her head back and clutched her flowers. *Pay attention to the photographer.*

Yet even as she tried, she was fully aware of Nicholas's hand on hers.

The photographer set up a few more poses. In

one Cara had to sit on Nicholas's knee. In another she had his jacket slung over her shoulder.

Nicholas smiled and posed, but he seemed aloof.

She got through it all and as soon as they were done, she fled the scene. She quickly found some jobs to do and kept herself busy and out of Nicholas's way.

Chapter Twelve

"I'd like to welcome everyone here tonight," Bert, Lorne's brother, was saying as people got themselves settled at their respective tables.

Thankfully Trista had the bridesmaid and the best man flanking them at the head table so Cara didn't have to sit beside Nicholas throughout the meal, as well. She couldn't forget the way her heart stuttered at the merest touch.

She had to get over this, she thought, angry at her runaway emotions. "Before we start, I'd like to ask Pastor Samuels to give a blessing on the meal."

The pastor came to the front. He'd already taken off his tie and looked far more relaxed and approachable than he had at the ceremony.

He looked over the head table, his eyes catching and holding each of theirs in turn, and Cara returned his smile. She reminded herself to talk to him about the sermon and thank him for his encouraging words.

"Welcome everyone, to this part of Lorne and Trista's wedding. Jesus blessed the couple in Cana with His presence at their wedding, and we pray that His presence may be felt here, too." He looked around at the gathering then bowed his head.

Cara followed suit. And as the pastor prayed she joined in, struggling to reach for peace.

She was here for Trista. She simply had to get over herself.

Dinner was a noisy affair with aunts and uncles, cousins and a few friends stopping at the table to talk to the married couple. Cara smiled and nodded, reminding people who she was.

By the time dessert arrived, her mouth was tired of smiling and the low-level headache dogging her all day had become a pounding, throbbing presence.

Then a tall, blond-haired man stopped in front of her and held out his hand. His smile exposed teeth that were extrawhite in contrast to his tanned skin.

"Cara Morrison. How are you?"

Cara glanced up, her mind struggling to place the handsome man.

"Tod. Tod Hanson," he prompted. "We went

on a couple of dates. I lived in Olds and we met at a football game."

And Cara remembered. "You took me to the symphony. In Calgary."

"And a movie. I didn't want you to think I was some kind of cultural snob."

Cara laughed. "That's right. That was fun."

Tod raised one eyebrow. "Was it? I had no idea you enjoyed yourself. You stopped returning my calls."

"I got busy." A flush warmed her cheeks and she was unwilling to admit that fear more than busyness had kept her away. He was attractive and fun and she couldn't understand what he saw in her. "So how do you know Lorne and Trista?"

"I'm a fill-in date for Trista's sister." He angled his head to one side, his smile growing. "Her boyfriend, my roommate, couldn't come. When I found out you were going to be here, I said I'd gladly take his place."

Cara's flush grew warmer. "Really?"

"Yeah. Really. And I'd really like to claim a dance later on."

"I think that might work," she said, forcing herself not to glance at Nicholas. Spending time with another guy would be good for her. Make her realize Nicholas wasn't the only fish in the sea.

"I'll catch you later." He pointed his finger at her, then winked and walked away.

Trista's brother walked to the podium, made a few jokes about his sister and then turned to Cara.

"I just noticed Tod talking to you, Cara. And I know there are a few other guys who have noticed you, as well. Cara, my dear men, is still single and still attractive. She works as a vet." He glanced at his paper and grinned. "Cara has been visiting Cochrane, the vet clinic for now, but rumor has it she's moving to Montreal soon. She used to live in Cochrane but before that, she and her mother traveled wherever the wind took them. So though she's single, she's a challenge to pin down." He gave her a quick grin. "Cara was also Trista's best friend when she lived here, which I understand is the longest time this peripatetic girl ever stayed in one place. Which explains how Nicholas Chapman managed to nab her. But only for a time, gentlemen, only for a time." This netted her another grin, which she gamely returned. "But enough about Cara. She is going to talk about my sister and hopefully give us some new insights into the inner workings of Trista's early years."

Cara drew a quick breath, sent up a prayer for strength and picked up her glass.

In one of her classes, her prof had said the

number one fear most people had was of public speaking.

She wanted to add a caveat to that. Public speaking in front of an old fiancé in a setting that was supposed to have been their wedding created a stress level beyond that basic fear.

Just pretend he's not here. Don't look at him, don't acknowledge him. This is about Trista and your tribute to her.

She glanced nervously around the gathering, her hands clammy on her glass as all faces turned to her. She wished Uncle Alan and Aunt Lori would have stayed. They could have been her two-person cheering section.

Help me not to mess up in front of Nicholas, she prayed. *Help me not to get nervous.*

She cleared her throat and dove in.

"When I first met Trista I was a gawky teenager, new to the community and new to the school. I was in eleventh grade and had been in as many schools in as many grades. I wasn't looking forward to starting all over." She turned to Trista and smiled. "I remember standing by the fence, looking around the groups of people and wondering where I would fit in when this bouncy, cheerful girl bopped up to me and asked me my name. I was entranced by her confidence and so thankful I could have kissed her."

"I know the feeling," Lorne piped in.

Cara waited for the general laughter following that comment to die down. "Trista taught me how to put on makeup, how to dress, how to do my hair and how to talk to guys—something that I struggled with."

"I can't believe that," Trista's brother called out.

More polite laughter.

"Lorne, I want you to know that Trista is a loyal, caring, warmhearted person. Trista stood up for me when I got picked on by kids who thought I was a bit strange because I'd never stayed long in one place." Cara's eyes were on Trista but she sensed Nicholas's intent gaze, as real as a touch—caught his puzzled frown. When they were together, she had kept comments about her past to minimal jokes, adopting a breezy tone as if none of it mattered. But it had, and in her desire to show Trista what her friendship meant, she had unwittingly exposed herself.

His attentiveness made her falter a moment, but she recovered. What did it matter what he knew about her now? Nothing she said would have an effect on their lives.

"Trista stood up for me as, for what seemed like the hundredth time, I navigated yet again unfamiliar ground of new schools and new people," Cara said, soldiering on. "She stood up for me when I needed a friend and, at times, a shoulder to cry on when I felt all alone. She lent me her clothes, her advice and helped me find my place. She stood by me through thick and thin and it's an honor to stand up for her now." She looked around the room. "Could you all join me in a toast to a beautiful bride, a dear friend and a loving wife."

"To Trista," was echoed around the tent.

As she walked back to the head table, her gaze unwittingly slipped past Trista.

Nicholas stared at her, his features now an enigmatic mask.

Cara sat down, her heart pounding in her chest.

"Nicholas Chapman, best friend of the groom and also single, is well-known to most of us. He's lived here all his life, though the past number of years more than half his time is spent raking in the money on offshore rigs and, lately, Kuwait. According to Lorne he's hoping to retire early so he can sit and count his ill-gotten gains." Bert threw Nicholas a mischievous grin. "But for now he's still working. So, girls, if you want to catch him, you've got about a week until he ships out again, so no dilly-dallying."

He stepped aside to polite laughter as Nicholas made his way to the podium.

"Good evening," Nicholas said, looking around the gathering. "I've known Lorne since I was a kid. I've got more memories than we've got time but if you want to know particulars about the night the cows got into his dad's wheat crop, or how the sugar got into his brother's motorcycle's gas tank, or why the windmill stopped working, or how the graffiti got on the number two overpass…well, suffice it to say I'll be here all night." He winked at Lorne. "Trista, you and Lorne are meant for each other. I know Lorne will be a loving, caring husband. That he will treat you with respect and consideration. That he will put your needs first and that he will be a support to you in your faith journey." He lifted his glass. "To Lorne."

Cara kept her eyes down as Nicholas talked, his voice pulling at old memories. Yet his words cut when he spoke of Lorne putting Trista's needs first.

He didn't see it, she thought. He didn't see what he had done to her and her headache increased.

Cara leaned close to Trista. "I have to go get my purse. I'll just be a minute."

"You okay?" Trista asked. "You look a bit pale."

"Headache. I'll be okay."

Cara got up and left the tent, thankful for the cooling evening air. She deliberately took her time walking to the house, her frustration with Nicholas slowly easing with each step she took.

Why should his words bother her? Just because he recognized that Lorne would put Trista first, didn't mean he'd do the same.

She found her purse in the room they had changed in, popped a couple of aspirin and left, closing the door behind her.

Across the hall, the door to Nicholas's room was open. Curiosity drew her to the doorway and she took a quick look in. Pictures of various rodeo cowboys hung on the wall right above a trophy he must have received competing in a rodeo.

A small pair of cowboy boots sat on a shelf above his bed. His, she presumed. Old school pictures hung on one wall beside some older pictures of what seemed to be his grandparents. Beside them, a wedding photo of his parents, which surprised her. Though Nicholas never talked about his mother, he obviously still cared about her.

As she looked around the room filled with the detritus of a life lived in one place, a sense of homesickness nudged her.

The only place she had ever stayed long enough to collect memorabilia was at her aunt and uncle's place in Cochrane. And even then, the only things she had in her bedroom were a few mementos from the two years she went to high school here.

Once again she was struck by the fact that

Nicholas had history. With a wistful smile, she turned away and went downstairs.

She closed the door of the house behind her, and just as she headed down the porch stairs, a tall figure loomed in the dark. She stifled a startled scream before she realized it was Nicholas.

"Are you okay?" He had one hand slung up in his pocket, the other tapped the seam of his pants.

She remembered too well the touch of that hand on her hip, the other on hers. And how, for a moment, she had felt safe.

"I have a bit of a headache," she said. "I was heading back to the party."

"Trista sent me looking for you. They're about to do the first dance."

Cara nodded her acknowledgment of her obligations even as her heart fluttered at the thought of dancing with Nicholas.

But before she left, he caught her hand and turned her back to him. In the gathering dusk, his glittering eyes were focused on her like a laser.

"You never told me it was hard for you coming here."

She shrugged aside his comment, adopting a breezy tone to let him know it didn't matter. "That was way in the past. I only wanted Trista to know what she did for me, that's all."

Thankfully he didn't say anything, but as they

walked back, he kept his hand in the small of her back, sending tiny shivers dancing up her spine. But she didn't move away.

The music had already started when they made their way back into the tent. Trista and Lorne were already twirling around on the dance floor, eyes only for each other. Cara watched them with a smile. They made such a perfect couple.

The music changed, and Trista turned and beckoned to her. That was the signal for Cara and Nicholas to join them.

"Shall we?" Nicholas held his hand out to her, and she placed hers in his. This time his hand was warm and hers cold. His fingers tightened as he gently drew her into his arms.

Cara's hand trembled as she laid it on his shoulder, and her heart fluttered out an irregular beat. She tried to keep herself distant from him, but then his hand on her waist slipped around and drew her closer.

Once again she was struck by how right it felt to be in his arms. As if she had been lost for a time and was now where she belonged.

She closed her eyes, allowing herself to enjoy the moment. Then giving into an impulse, she slipped her arm around his back, and laid her head on his shoulder.

She drew in a long, slow breath, and eased it out, hardly daring to breathe.

Forgive me, Lord, she prayed, as her arm tightened around him. *He still means so much to me.*

His breath fanned her hair, and then to her surprise, she heard him whisper her name.

"What is it?" she whispered back.

"I missed you." He words came out in a sigh, warm on her ear. "I didn't want to, but I do."

Though he whispered the words, they thundered in her ear, creating a storm of confusion. She thought of how aloof he had looked the past hour, of how he kept his distance.

"I thought you were angry with me," she said, keeping her head on his shoulder.

"I was. I was angry because I couldn't help how I still feel about you."

She thought again of the kiss they had shared. What was happening between them? And what was she supposed to do about it?

Time and time again she was confronted with her old feelings for Nicholas. And somehow, since coming back to Cochrane, they had changed, grown deeper, more intense.

"I couldn't stop thinking about what you said the other day," he said. "About how you had planned our wedding." He drew back to look at her face. "How you had seen us with a future."

"At one time, I did."

"I did, too."

He spun her around in time to the music and then spoke again, his voice deep, intense.

"I can't get you out of my mind, Cara. I thought I could, but you keep haunting me."

His words sang through her soul. He felt the same way she did, she thought, as her heart took a long, slow dive.

She leaned back a bit as Nicholas made another turn, the twinkling minilights softening the lean line of his jaw.

"I keep thinking about you, too," she returned, holding his earnest gaze.

"I don't know about you, but I'm tired of just thinking. Do you think there is a chance for us?"

Cara nestled her head against his neck, her fluttering heart now thundering out its beat.

"Maybe," she whispered back. It wasn't much, but for now it was all she could give him. She was still afraid of him and the emotions he easily resurrected in her.

Yet the thought of being without him seemed harder to bear than the thought of being with him.

Then, to her surprise, his lips brushed her temple, then her cheek. She closed her eyes, letting him beguile her.

Then it seemed all too soon the music stopped and the dance was over. Nicholas gently drew back, and fingered a strand of hair away from her face.

"We need to talk," he said. "But not here and now." He released her but he still held her hands. "Will you go out with me? Tuesday?"

Cara couldn't look away and knew she couldn't say no.

"I want to get things cleared up between us," he continued. "I feel like we didn't finish our last conversation."

That was because she didn't think there was anything left to say.

"Okay. Where should we meet?" she asked.

His eyes looked dark, and as Cara held his gaze awareness arced between them. "Would you be willing to come here?"

She nodded, then drifted toward him and a sudden tap on her shoulder pulled her back to reality. She blinked, then turned.

"I've come to collect my dance." Tod stood in front of her, grinning as he held his hand out.

Cara looked back at Nicholas, almost hoping he would rescue her. But he stepped aside and gestured for Tod to take over.

Tod took her in his arms. "I've been looking forward to this," he said. "Hoping maybe we could pick up where we left off."

My, wasn't she the popular ex-girlfriend

tonight, she thought, with a touch of cynicism as Tod twirled her around the dance floor.

She only listened with half an ear to Tod, gave him an occasional distracted smile. Tod was better looking but as she danced with him, her eyes continually sought and found Nicholas. And each time she saw him, he was watching her with an enigmatic expression on his face.

When the dance was over, she begged off and went to get a drink from the lemonade fountain. She looked for Nicholas and saw him standing to one side of the party, talking to someone she didn't recognize. He laughed, patted the man on the shoulder and moved on, mixing with the people. People he knew and had known since he was a child.

He belongs here. The thought settled with certainty. *This is his home and his community.*

She sat a few dances out, chatted with a few people, but her eyes kept finding his.

Each time their eyes met, she knew she hadn't imagined that surreal moment on the dance floor.

And anticipation over what would happen on Tuesday seemed to rise with each shared look across the room, each light brush of his hand as he passed her.

What would he talk about?

And would it change her plans?

Chapter Thirteen

Cara's eyes flicked over the church bulletin but she wasn't reading anything she saw.

Every time a man walked down the aisle of the church her heart started up. But so far Nicholas hadn't shown up.

This morning, when she got up in time to go to church with her aunt and uncle, Aunt Lori barely managed to hide her surprise.

Though she'd crawled into bed at three-thirty after helping the families clean up, exchanging glances with Nicholas the entire time, she couldn't sleep.

Too many thoughts were clamoring for attention. Between the sermon from the pastor at the wedding and Nicholas's sudden confession, she didn't know which way to turn.

On the one hand God promised that He'd never leave her alone. And on the other, she ran the risk of letting that promise be taken over by what Nicholas might want to talk to her about.

Did the two need to be mutually exclusive? Was she looking for signs where she should simply be looking to renew her relationship with God and let everything else fall where it may?

So she came to church, hoping to find nourishment for a soul that had kept itself far from God too long.

And hoping Nicholas would show.

The worship team came to the front and started playing a song Cara remembered from her earlier years. By the third verse, Cara had let the words of the song soothe her anticipation and put it where it should be.

The peace promised her in the song stole over her.

"Hey there."

The deep voice shivered through her, shaking her newfound serenity.

She turned to Nicholas. "Hey yourself."

He sat down beside her and, ignoring her aunt's raised eyebrows and her uncle's puzzled frown, she gave him a careful smile.

"You got up early for being out so late last night," he said quietly, leaning close to her.

"So did you," she whispered back. "Did everyone leave after I did?"

"Pretty much."

And suddenly there was nothing more to say. Either they moved directly into what Nicholas wanted to talk about or they bided their time until they could do it properly.

One step at a time, Cara told herself. She wasn't sure what lay ahead. Her plans were still in place and she had no solid reason to change them.

So why did she feel another possibility glimmering over the horizon?

Keep your focus on the pastor, she reminded herself, drawing comfort and encouragement from what he said.

Her soul drank it all in, yearning for more.

As they rose to sing the final song, a sense of contentment overrode her other feelings. She didn't know what lay ahead, but she knew God held her life in His hands.

As the notes from the final song faded away, Nicholas turned to her. "I'll call you tomorrow. Make arrangements for Tuesday, okay?"

She held his gaze and nodded as expectation quivered between them.

"Those bales are heavy," Dale said, leaning back against the bale wagon piled high with sweet-smelling hay bales. "Hay is looking good."

Nicholas took a long sip of the iced tea his father had brought out, his eyes wandering over the tight, round bales still dotting the field. The summer smell of warm hay permeated the air, creating a feeling of well-being.

"Did you check the heifers before you came here?" Nicholas asked.

His father nodded. "Crackerjack bunch of animals. That guy in Montana will be thrilled." His father pushed his hat back on his head and took another sip of lemonade. "Is that Morrison girl going to do the test?"

"Not sure, Dad." Nicholas sighed, then glanced up at his father. "Why do you talk that way about her?"

His father blew out his breath and took another sip of iced tea. "You're not getting involved with her again, are you?"

Nicholas's mind ticked back the wedding—the moment of closeness with Cara. Was he getting involved with her? But he didn't answer his father.

"You still never told me much about that day you two came riding back on Two Bits," his father said.

"Like I told you, my horse spooked, she got dumped and I was worried about her." Nicholas conveniently glossed over the kiss they had shared. The kiss that had rocked his world.

"And the wedding? You've been walking around in some kind of daze since then."

And it was a good thing his father had gone to that rodeo at Sundre the day of the wedding. Nicholas said he wanted his dad's help but now Nicholas realized his absence was for the best. His father had missed his dance with Cara.

He didn't need his father ragging on him about Cara. Not when he wasn't sure himself where things were going and what was happening. For now, he was taking things one day at a time.

"Is she starting to get to you?" Dale pressed.

"I've got things under control," was all Nicholas said, squinting at the sun as his narrowed eyes followed the contours of the land. He knew every hummock, had ridden through every valley and moved cows over every hill.

And he hoped one day he could show his own son or daughter the land that had been in the Chapman family for so many generations. He wondered what that child would look like.

Wondered who would be standing beside him.

"She's a distraction," his father continued. He just wouldn't give up.

"What do you mean?" Nicholas pulled his attention back to his dad.

"You said yourself after she left that she doesn't get your commitment to the ranch. Doesn't understand how it's in your blood and in your soul."

Nicholas had thought that at one time. But after

that aborted ride into the hills with Trista and Lorne, he wasn't so sure. As he and Cara rode and talked, he sensed she understood his attraction to the land and history that permeated his life.

"Cara left you once before, Nicholas. Not only left you, ran out on you without a word. Don't fall for her again. I can see how she looks at you. She still feels something for you. You've got to keep your eye on the prize," Dale continued. "A few more years and the ranch will be where it should be. That's a sacrifice worth making."

Nicholas thought of what Cara had said on the ride back to the ranch. How she wondered why he worked a job he didn't like when his heart was so obviously here.

He thought of how interested she seemed when he told her his family's history. How she seemed to appreciate the roots that held him firmly to this place.

And his mind cast back to Sunday morning in church when he sat beside her and how he felt, for the first time in his life, willing to step into an unknown. To stop doing the never-ending work bringing in money that was never enough.

Because each time they paid off one loan, it seemed to open the way to previously unavailable possibilities.

"I sometimes wonder if I have that in me anymore, Dad," Nicholas said finally.

His father frowned. "What do you mean?"

"You weren't in church on Sunday," Nicholas said, folding his arms over his chest. "But the pastor read a piece from Philippians that I've been thinking about the past day or two. 'I have learned the secret of being content in any and every situation, whether well fed or hungry, whether living in plenty or want.' And I got to thinking. I'm not content. Not content at work and I'm not content when I'm on the ranch. There is always one more thing to buy, one more piece of machinery to fix, one more loan to pay down. Money is flowing in, but it's not making me content."

"If you keep working that'll change."

The note of desperation in his father's voice caught Nicholas's attention.

"We have a plan," his father continued. "We sell the heifers, get a steady market for our breeding stock. Then we'll be in better shape. But we need to stick to the plan. Don't let that Morrison girl distract you."

Nicholas was tired of his father talking about Cara, but he knew if he defended her, his father wouldn't quit. Besides, he wasn't sure what was happening between them, but he knew that some spark of what they had before still lingered.

Maybe he was wrong about Cara, maybe he was a fool, but he sensed she felt the same.

"I better get back to work." He pushed himself away from the tractor. "I want to have the hay off the field by tomorrow."

When he and Cara would be seeing each other.

After that he had to get the heifers—their ticket to the next step up in the ranch's economic fortunes—tested and ready to ship.

And after that?

He had a job waiting and yet…

For the first time in years he was willing to put a question mark on his future.

Could he do it? Could he make the sacrifice Cara asked him to make all those years ago?

Would Cara change her mind about him if he did?

Chapter Fourteen

Pink shirt? Blue shirt?

Cara held one in front of her, then another. Nicholas was coming in ten minutes. She'd barely had time to wash the dust out of her hair from her last job and now she had to figure out what to wear.

She would have called Trista, but her friend was on her honeymoon and Cara didn't think she'd appreciate a phone call asking for fashion advice.

Cara wrinkled her nose, tossed aside the pink shirt and slipped on the blue one. Done. Now she had to figure out what to do with her still-damp hair. Ponytail? Let it hang loose?

Nicholas had called yesterday and asked if she'd be willing to go riding again. She had reluctantly agreed, knowing she had to for her sake. And Nicholas.

Nicholas wouldn't put her in danger, she thought. She knew that as surely as she knew the color of her own eyes.

She let go of her hair and decided to let it hang loose. Nicholas had said once that he liked it down. Besides, when she was working she always pulled it back in a serviceable ponytail. And she wasn't working tonight. Bill was covering the calls.

A bit of makeup, a quick fluff of her bangs and she was done.

Aunt Lori stood by the kitchen table, a tea towel slung over her shoulder, paging through a magazine. Behind her the kitchen counter was still stacked with the dinner dishes that Cara had offered to do half an hour ago.

Obviously her aunt had gotten distracted again.

She looked up when Cara came into the room. "You look nice."

"Where's Uncle Alan? I thought he said he was going to help you with the dishes." Cara slipped her denim jacket on over her shirt and pulled her hair free.

"He went to the clinic." Aunt Lori turned another page in the magazine and then put it on the table, folding a corner of the page down. "I was looking for this recipe."

"Why don't I help do the dishes a minute?"

Cara said, glancing at the clock. She wasn't early enough to finish the job, but if she could get her aunt started, hopefully they would get done.

But Aunt Lori waved her off. "Your uncle said he wouldn't be at the clinic long. He'll help me when he comes back."

"Why is Uncle Alan at the clinic anyway? Surely he's not covering calls for Bill?"

Aunt Lori shook her head as she looked up from the magazine. "He said something about meeting that new vet, Gordon Moen, at the clinic. I guess he came in today and wanted to see the clinic as soon as possible."

"Neither Bill nor Anita said anything to me when I was at the clinic this afternoon."

"They must have forgot."

Cara frowned. She wasn't a partner in the clinic and she was only helping temporarily, but surely she could have been given this rather important piece of information.

"Maybe I should stop at the clinic on my way to Nicholas's."

"Do whatever you want, my dear," Aunt Lori said, tapping her chin with her finger. "What do you think of skewers for supper tomorrow? If I grill them they would be fairly healthy, I'm thinking."

"Do whatever you want, my dear," Cara returned.

"Oh, speaking of not passing information on…" Aunt Lori gave her a guilty smile. "I got a phone call from that place in Montreal where you'll be working." This was said with a grimace as if Aunt Lori didn't want to consider this. "They want you to call them as soon as possible."

Uncertainty slipped into Cara. She knew that each day she spent here in Cochrane brought her one day closer to her departure.

It was just the past few days she had preferred not to think about that.

"You're still taking that job?" Aunt Lori asked.

"The job is a fantastic opportunity," Cara said slowly, considering her own words but not as convinced as she used to be. "The pay is almost twice what I've been making the past few years. I can pay you back—"

Her aunt slashed the air with her hand. "How many times do I have to tell you? Your uncle and I don't want that money back. It was a gift of love and you just have to take it."

Cara heard the words on one level, but still struggled with the idea on another.

"Love is freely given," her aunt continued. "It doesn't require anything in return."

"I know," she said quietly, though she still wasn't entirely convinced. "But the job will also give me a chance to travel. Like you always said I should."

"That was your uncle Alan's advice."

Cara frowned. "What do you mean?"

Aunt Lori tilted her head, scratching the side of her neck. "I think, in his heart, he was a bit like your mother. The only reason we've stayed here as long as we have is because I told him I wanted roots."

"So you think traveling is a bad idea?"

"I think traveling can be good at one point in your life, but I also think there comes a time when you need to make yourself a part of something. Get connected to a community. It's hard to nourish your faith when you don't have community—when you don't have roots." Aunt Lori gave a light laugh. "I was very happy when you and Nicholas started dating and almost as sad as you when it was over. And now you're seeing him again. I think it's a good thing, regardless of what Uncle Alan might say."

Pleasure twinged through her. "We're not really seeing each other. It's just a ride up into the mountains."

Aunt Lori smiled, as if she didn't believe Cara's protestations. "Anyway, you have a good time."

Cara bent over and gave her aunt a quick kiss. "I hope to."

She wasn't going to dwell on the phone call she

had to make tomorrow or what Gordon's arrival might mean for her. And she decided she wasn't stopping at the clinic either.

Nicholas was waiting for her when she parked her car by the corrals. He wore his usual blue jeans and a blue shirt with a thin white stripe. Then she felt an opening sensation in her chest as she recognized his shirt.

Was it the one she had given him when they were dating?

"Nice shirt," she blurted out as he came near.

Nicholas gave her a crooked smile. "Thanks. An old girlfriend bought it for me."

She was right.

To hide her discomposure, she looked around the yard.

The arbor still stood beside the barn. Potted plants still hung from it and others were pushed up against it, creating a splash of color and whimsy.

"You didn't take it down yet," she said, tucking her hands in her pockets.

"It spruces up the yard," Nicholas said. He poked his thumb over his shoulder. "I've got the horses saddled up in the corral. I'd like you to walk your horse around a bit. Get used to him."

"Which one will I be riding?" she asked,

following him around the wooden fence of the corral.

"I thought I would put you on one of my dad's horses." He unlatched the gate and pushed it open to let her through. "I don't trust Two Bits after that spill you took the other day."

"It wasn't his fault," Cara said, waiting for Nicholas to latch the gate again. "He just got scared and I didn't have both my feet in the stirrups."

"Nice of you to give him an out, but I'm not taking any chances." His beguiling smile didn't help her equilibrium.

One of the horses nickered as they came near and Nicholas walked over and untied a tall, gray horse. "This horse is called Sammy. She used to be a pickup horse at the rodeo. Bulletproof. I would have put you on her the first time, but Dad had her at the neighbor's to get bred."

Cara surveyed the animal as Nicholas walked over with her. "A bit old to be a mother, don't you think?"

Nicholas handed her the reins. "I thought so, too, but Dad figures she could have a couple more colts yet."

Cara held her hand out to the horse, letting the mare get a whiff of her, then gently stroked the horse's nose. The mare stood stock-still, then blew out a breath.

"Just lead her around the corral a bit," Nicholas said, untying his horse, as well. "Let her get used to you—"

"And let me get used to her," Cara finished for him.

"That's about the size of it." Nicholas flashed her a grin, his teeth white against his tanned face.

Cara grasped the leather reins and started walking, the muffled thump of the horse's feet on the ground and the squeak of saddle leather the only sounds she heard. The sound of quiet contentment.

"Make her do a few turns, then make her stop and go," Nicholas called out.

Sammy responded to the smallest tug of the reins. When she brought the horse back to Nicholas, Cara felt more comfortable about getting on her back.

"So. Ready to head out?" Nicholas asked.

"I think so."

Nicholas helped her on the horse, adjusted the stirrups, tightened the cinch then tipped his hat back to look up at her. "You sure you're okay with this?"

She sensed an underlying tone to his question that had less to do with the horse and more to do with him.

She gave him a gentle smile and nodded. "Yeah. I'm sure."

His answering grin created a feeling of expectation. "Good. Then let's go."

He swung easily up on his horse and with a twist of his wrist had the horse turned and headed toward the gate. Without dismounting he leaned over and unlatched it, led his horse through, then waited while Cara followed before latching the gate again.

Then he set his hat more firmly on his head, clucked lightly and once again they rode out of the yard and across the open field.

She heard the bawl of a cow and turned in time to see a herd of about thirty black Angus heifers walking toward them, obviously curious.

Their hides gleamed in the sunlight, their uniform faces staring back at her.

"Nice bunch of heifers you got here," she called out.

Nicholas half turned in the saddle, looking back at her. Then he reined his horse in. He was looking at the heifers, as well, when she caught up to him. "They're doing great. If the guy in Montana likes them, it's a huge deal for the ranch."

Huge enough to make him stay instead of going out to work?

But Cara wisely kept the question to herself.

"You've been working hard on the bloodlines of this herd, haven't you?" Cara asked, remembering her uncle talking about trips to the Chapman ranch to artificially inseminate the growing herd with top-notch semen from prize-winning bulls.

Nicholas pushed his hat back on his head, leaning forward in the saddle. "You're looking at almost six years of breeding and culling. And a lot of money invested in good genetics."

"They look amazing," Cara said. Her comment earned her a quick smile.

"And once we run the tests, we're good to go." His horse blew, then stamped, and Nicholas straightened. "Two Bits is getting impatient. We should get going." He pointed with one hand to the trail. "We'll go the same way we went last time. We'll end up at the place where Trista and Lorne wanted their pictures taken. It's only about a twenty-minute ride from here."

"Sounds good to me." Cara's nervousness eased with each step of the horse and by the time they were back on the trail again, she relaxed. Every now and then Sammy would twitch her ears as if checking to see if she still sat on her back, but mostly her mount was content to plod along.

The quiet and cool of the approaching evening surrounded them as the horses climbed higher and higher. The creak of leather and the plod of the horses' hooves were the only sound in the utter stillness of the day.

Cara caught glimpses of the fields below them growing smaller the higher they went. Twenty minutes later, just as Nicholas had promised, they broke out into an open area.

"This is the end of the road," Nicholas said, bringing his horse to a stop. Cara's horse sidled up to him and stopped, as well. "We'll get off the horses here and tie them up. Then we can walk to the lookout point," Nicholas said, swinging off his saddle. Cara followed suit and a few minutes later Nicholas was leading her through the small clearing to an opening in the trees.

They got to the edge and the ground fell away from them.

The tree-covered hillside sloped away, meeting hayfields and pasture well below them. Beyond that lay the creek Nicholas had pointed out the last time they had ridden the trail up here. Beyond that the land rose again, green-skirted hills meeting blue and gray jagged peaks softened by caps of snow gleaming against a blue sky.

A wave of dizziness washed over her at the vast expanse of land. "Tell me again which part is yours?" she asked, breathless with the wonder and beauty of it all.

"The fields along the river belong to us, and

through that cut in the hills are the high pastures where the other cows are grazing."

Cara hugged herself, letting her gaze roam over the space. "It's absolutely beautiful," she breathed. "I don't know if I want to leave."

"I know the feeling," Nicholas said, sitting down on the ground.

Cara hesitated a moment, then followed suit. And, to her surprise, Nicholas moved closer and she didn't move away.

His arm brushed hers and she caught the scent of horse mixed with hay and the faintest hint of soap.

The smell of Nicholas, she thought.

She turned her attention back to the view.

"I don't know how you can leave this," she said, wrapping her arms around her knees.

Nicholas didn't reply and she wished she could take her ill-timed comment back. It was that leaving that had caused the tension that sang between them last time.

Then he turned to her and grinned. "And I don't know how you can work in a lab when I know that you love working with animals."

His comment spoke to her doubts. Since she had started working for her uncle, she felt anchored. Secure. As if the land and the people and the community were drawing her into themselves and giving her the home she missed when she was working in Vancouver.

"I do love it here. I feel like I can breathe."

"So why go?"

He spoke the words lightly, but they clung to Cara, mining her own doubts.

"There isn't room for me at the clinic. This new vet is here, Uncle Alan is feeling better and I'm already starting to feel redundant." She tried to keep her voice as light as Nicholas did, but her own uncertainties hovered over her future.

And her changing feelings for Nicholas.

"I wasn't just talking about the clinic," Nicholas said quietly, a wealth of meaning in his voice.

"I know." She turned to him and as their eyes met, her concerns receded. "And what about you? Do you have to go?"

Nicholas sighed as he leaned his elbows on his knees. "Unfortunately, yes."

The finality of his statement resurrected her wavering. "Will there come a time when you don't have to leave? When the ranch can hold its own?"

Nicholas didn't answer right away and once again she wondered if she had entered forbidden territory.

"I'm hoping." He looked at her, then to her surprise, reached up and cupped her cheek in his hand. As her heart billowed and expanded in her chest, he leaned closer and brushed his lips over hers. "I'm really hoping."

Cara swallowed as his hope became hers.

He pulled back, tracing her mouth with his thumb. "So, Cara Morrison, now what?" he asked, articulating her own question.

"I'm not sure," she said, her voice breathless.

"We never had much of a chance to talk the last time we were together."

Cara wasn't sure where he was going, but he guessed he referred to the conversation that had initiated the breakup.

Nicholas moved his thumb over her lips again, then gave her a careful smile. "When I found out that you had actually made wedding plans, it made me rethink all the questions I'd had when you left the first time. Why couldn't you wait for me to come back so we could make our own wedding plans?"

The whisper of the leaves around them filled the silence following his simple question as she struggled to find the right response—to find the right words to articulate her hurt and betrayal.

Cara leaned away from him to give herself what space she could. "Why did you leave even though I asked you to stay?" Begged him to stay, but she wasn't bringing up that humiliation again.

Nicholas sighed and lowered his hand. "I told

you then and I'm telling you now. The ranch needed the money."

"And now? Does the ranch still need the money?" The words fell between them like a glove being thrown down.

I need to know, Cara thought, justifying her repeat of the question she'd asked him a few moments ago. *I need to know where things are going before I follow him down that path again.*

Nicholas looked away and Cara followed his gaze, her eyes tracing the lines of the hills and valleys. She let herself get drawn into the vast, open spaces stretching out and away from where they sat.

"This ranch is part of my identity. Part of who I am and where I came from. Some Chapman sweat and even some Chapman blood is in every square inch of this place. Those are my roots, my heritage and I have to protect that."

His passion resonated with the very thing she had been looking for in her life. Yet she heard an underlying tone that disconcerted her.

"Because of your mother?" Cara spoke the question cautiously. Nicholas seldom spoke of his mother. The other time they went riding, she thought he hovered on the verge of telling her more.

Nicholas got up, walking toward the cliff

overlooking the valley. "This is all Chapman land, slowly built up over the years. When my mother left my father she got enough of the ranch in the divorce settlement that it bordered on being broke. She had no right to this land. She had no right to not only break my father's heart, but to almost break this ranch."

"And now she's gone," Cara said quietly.

When she and Nicholas were first dating, the only information she got from him was that Barb had left his father and that she had died shortly after remarrying.

"And the money with her. So I keep working," Nicholas said. "And my work on the rigs is bringing this ranch back to where it should be." He turned back to her. "I'm not doing this just for myself," he added. "I'm also doing this for my father."

Cara held his gaze and she heard it again. The faint note of urgency. As if something else was going on. And then it became clear.

"Why are you doing this for him?"

"Because he's had a hard life. Because he doesn't deserve what my mother did to him. I need to protect him."

"From what?" Cara's frustration with Dale Chapman and Nicholas merged. "He's a grown man, he doesn't need your protection."

"What are you trying to say?" His voice grew

quiet, but carried a weight that made Cara want to back down.

But she wasn't the quiet, soft-spoken person she'd been before. She'd found her own way, lived on her own and made her own decisions. Nicholas had to see what was going on because it seemed no one else dared tell him.

"All the work you do, all the money you make, is poured into this ranch. And that is admirable. But did your father do the same with what was given to him?" She paused, wondering if she dared venture into the place she was heading. But if anything was going to happen between them, if anything was to be rebuilt, it had to be on a different foundation than before. Or else it would fall as easily as before.

"He worked for this place, too," Nicholas said, turning away from her. But he didn't sound as confident as he had before. As if her comment had seeded the tiniest bit of doubt in his view of his father.

"Did he?" A tiny voice cautioned Cara as she struggled to find the right words. Her intention was not to put his father down, but to give him the viewpoint of an outsider looking in. "He spent a lot of time on the road going to his rodeos, didn't he?"

"Yeah. He loved doing it."

"Don't you think you made it easy for him to continue doing that?"

"How so?" His question sounded defensive and Cara fought the urge to change the subject.

"I wonder if, by working, you enable him to keep doing something that doesn't benefit the ranch. He doesn't spend as much time on this ranch as you do and it seems to me the bulk of the work gets done when you're home."

Nicholas shot her a look that would have pierced her any other time, but they had come to an important crossroads in their relationship and she had to forge on. She stood and walked closer to him.

"When I broke our engagement, I felt as if you chose working the rigs over me. And when you made that choice, in my eyes, it also seemed that you chose your father over me. You were choosing to make the ranch viable and easy to work for him. Your priority was him. So if you think I'm attacking your father, you're wrong. I'm just bringing up my view of the situation."

"I told you, I work because the ranch needs the money," Nicholas said with a weary sigh. "I got tired of watching my father fight with bills and bill collectors. Got tired of fixing fences with baler twine instead of being able to afford new boards. I promised myself I would do what I could to help him out. And there was no way

I was bringing another woman, my future wife, onto the ranch until I was set up to give her the support my mother didn't get."

"What do you mean?"

"I know my mother left because money was always so tight. I didn't want to run that risk again. My dangerous work allows me to put money into the ranch and spend time here, as well."

"But not as much as you like."

Nicholas blew out a sigh. "This is reality, Cara. My work brings in much-needed money. I refuse to constantly worry about which bill to pay and which one to let ride. I don't want to live like that, Cara. And I know you don't either."

"What are you trying to say?" A chill feathered down her spine as the old shame slipped back into her life.

He knew little from her past because shame had kept her tight-lipped about her life before moving in with her wealthy aunt and uncle.

"I remember that brand-new car you tooled around town with when you were in high school. You always wore the best clothes and could afford to do what you wanted. I know Alan paid for your education. You've had it pretty easy living with your aunt and uncle."

Anger sparked at his easy assumption. "But

you don't know what my life was like before that."

Nicholas turned to face her square on. "No. I don't. You never say much about that."

She heard the challenge in his voice and before she could stop herself, her anger made her spill the words out.

"You think I don't know what doing without is like? You think I've had it so incredibly easy? My mother was so intent on living the way she wanted that it didn't matter to her what I wore or what I ate." Cara took a breath to stop herself but it was as if the words, so long suppressed, were drawn out by the way Nicholas looked at her. "While I lived with my mother I missed meals. I had to pack my stuff in garbage bags because we were getting evicted from a motel. I learned how to make a pound of hamburger stretch over four meals for two. I lived in a motel. I lived in a trailer park and even a tent on a campground. An adventure, my mother told me—" Her voice broke and she pressed a hand on her lips, halting the flow of memories.

She shouldn't have let him get her so angry. She was telling him things she'd never told Aunt Lori and Uncle Alan.

Though she loved her mother, she struggled with guilt as she tried putting the shame of that part of her life behind her.

And when her mother died, her disloyalty and guilt were compounded.

"Cara, I'm sorry—"

Cara held her hand up to stop him. "The last thing I want is your pity. It's just that you made me angry. Thinking you have the monopoly on struggling and doing without. Thinking that money will fix all that's wrong in your life."

The only sound in the ensuing silence was the riffling of a benevolent breeze through the leaves of the trees and the sigh of her horse as she shifted her weight to another foot.

After a few minutes Nicholas spoke.

"I never knew, Cara. And though you don't want my pity, I want to tell you that I'm sorry for assuming your life was easy. I wish you would have told me sooner."

Cara ran her hand up and down one arm, staring over the hills lying below them. The hills belonging to Nicholas and his father. The land that had been in their family for five generations.

She wondered if he realized how much she envied him his roots and his stability. His history.

"Money was never that important to me," she continued. "Even though I grew up without it. I never wanted a fancy car or nice clothes, though I did enjoy them." She turned to him and caught his hands in hers. "I've lived with and I've lived without. And what made the times in my life when I had money more significant was the fact that I was cared for. The money was one of my aunt and uncle's expressions of love and sacrifice." She held his gaze, willing him to understand. "I would gladly have traded that car in, lost all the clothes, given up the paid-for education, just to have my mother back. Just to have her spend some time with me and see her eyes shine when she saw me."

Nicholas's gaze softened and he squeezed her hands back. "I'm sorry, Cara. I never knew."

She gave him a wan smile. "Just for the record, you're the only person I've ever told this to. Neither Trista nor my aunt and uncle know how poorly we lived all those years." Cara's knees wobbled and she lowered herself to the grass once again.

"Why haven't you told them?" Nicholas moved and sat down beside her.

Cara wrapped her arms around her knees and drew in a long, slow breath as if preparing herself. "I knew what they thought of my mother. Uncle Alan didn't particularly care for her and I also knew he was ashamed of her." She paused, the old guilt and the old confusion returning. "But she was my mother and I loved her. And yet…"

"You didn't know how to love her."

Cara rocked slowly back and forth as her

emotions returned to the old, endless circling between disloyalty and love. "Yeah. I guess you would know about that."

"I used to think God would punish me for hating my mother. For wishing she was dead. Then when she did die…" His voice trailed off and Cara placed her hand on his arm. "When she did die, I thought God was punishing me for sure."

"I don't know if God operates that way," Cara said. "I've had my own grievances with Him, but I'm slowly finding out not everything is about me. Sometimes it's simply about the choices that people make and their consequences."

"And what about your choices, Cara?"

"Now it's my turn to wonder what you mean."

Nicholas reached out and ran a callused finger down her cheek. "What choices are you going to make in the next week? What about your job?"

Did she dare pin all her hopes and dreams on the man standing in front of her?

"I don't know what to do," she said finally. "Especially when it seems like things are changing between us."

Nicholas raised his finger to her lips and as he traced their outline, he gave her a rueful smile. "I don't know what's happening either, Cara. I feel like we're the same people and yet not. I feel like we're both in different places making decisions with new information. I don't think we're heading in the same direction as we were before. But I like to think we can go in that direction together."

Cara held his gaze, her own heart lifting in response to his comment. Had things truly changed to bring them both to the same place in this relationship? Was Nicholas really willing to make different choices?

Was she?

Even as she wanted to let go of her worries and concerns, a question still hovered. A fear she couldn't articulate.

Please, Lord, she prayed, *help us through this uncertainty.* Then she gave Nicholas a cautious smile. Reached out and caressed his face, tracing his own smile.

"I guess we'll have to wait and see then, won't we?"

Then he leaned closer and caught her lips in a warm, satisfying kiss.

Nicholas held the phone, his boss's phone number up on the screen. Did he dare make this phone call? Could he quit now?

One more year of work would pay off the tractor and give them a partial down payment on a parcel of land coming up for sale.

Stick with the plan, his father had urged.

But the thought of being gone again cut him to the core. Because he wouldn't just be leaving the ranch, he'd be leaving Cara.

He thought back to their moment on the hill. The things they had talked about. The honesty they'd both displayed, so unlike the first time they were together.

She said that money didn't matter to her. Yet the idea that his mother had left because of the tight financial situation was so ingrained in him, he couldn't shift his thoughts in the direction Cara had gone.

He walked to the window of his bedroom. From here he could see his father working in the round pen, training his newest horse. He'd picked up the bay at the auction mart while Nicholas was out piling up hay bales with the tractor.

He'd never resented his father his hobby. But, as Cara had said, it required time and dedication that took his father away from the ranch.

Nicholas's eyes drifted to the tractor sitting in the yard. Last year they'd had to put a new motor in. His father, in a rush to feed the cows so he could get to the auction mart, had used too much ether and blown the engine.

It took Nicholas a month of work to fix the tractor. Had he been home to run the tractor for the cows himself, he would have had to work one less month.

You enable your father. Cara's comment slipped into his mind and behind that, Lorne's— *Take a chance. Love is a risk, but I think it's a risk worth taking.*

Nicholas spun away from the window, wishing he could stifle all the voices running through his head.

He walked back to his bed and picked up the Bible again and reread the passage from Philippians, chapter 4. He let the words encourage him and soak into his life. When he had read it a number of times, he lowered his head and prayed for wisdom and strength to do the right thing.

Then he went outside.

His father was done with his horse and sat perched on a pail in the tack shed, braiding a lead rope. The shed was well stocked and neat as a pin. Neatly coiled ropes hung on the wall. Brushes and currycombs, hoof picks and trimming tools all had their place.

Across the far wall, five saddles hung on their respective saddle trees. One of them was the roping saddle his father had won. The other four were custom-made for his father.

Paid for by his father's horse trading, supposedly, but Nicholas knew a portion of the money he earned went into his father's hobby.

Nicholas brushed away the traitorous thought. He had made his own choices. No one was putting a gun to his head to go out and work. Nicholas would be lying if he said he didn't benefit from the high wages he got paid.

Since talking to Cara, he kept seeing his father's role in the ranch in a different light. He looked at what his father did through Cara's eyes and he realized that, to some degree, Cara was right.

"How's the new horse?" Nicholas asked, picking up a brush that had fallen to the ground.

"He's a bit jumpy, but he's willing and eager. He needs a bit of work, but then they all do." Dale gave Nicholas a wink. "Time and miles. That's what makes a mediocre horse good. Time and miles."

And his father spent enough of both on his horses, Nicholas thought.

"So, I've been penciling a few things out." Nicholas ran his thumb over the soft bristles of the brush, remembering how much he loved brushing his own horse after a long ride. Remembering how he seldom went riding anymore. "After we sell these heifers, I'm thinking I'll stay at home."

"So how do you figure that would work?" his father asked, his hands working the rope, his movements slower now.

"The ranch is coming along. We wouldn't get as much money as we used to, but we'd get by. And I'd be home more."

"You don't have to worry about me," Dale said. "I manage fine while you're gone."

"But I don't." Nicholas sighed. "I've got a fancy truck with all the options paid for by my work. We're accumulating land and vehicles and for what?"

Dale's set the rope aside and, resting his hands on his knees, looked up at Nicholas again. "You know one of the reasons your mom left was because we were broke all the time?"

Nicholas crossed his arms over his chest, his mind going back to what Cara had said. "Maybe Cara is different."

"We back to that Morrison girl again? Are you forgetting how hard it was when she dumped you?"

Nicholas's frustration with his father took wings. "Why are you so determined to think the worst of her? What has she ever done to you?"

"Dumped my son."

"But that was my pain, Dad. You didn't need to take it on."

Dale glared at Nicholas. "It was the same pain I went through. And you know why I went through it? Because it was Audra, Cara's mother, that convinced your mother to leave."

"What are you saying?" Nicholas frowned at his father, who nodded.

"Audra Morrison blew into town one day. Met up with your mother and they got to talking. Barb got to complaining. Next thing you know Audra's convincing Barb that she doesn't need to stay with me. That she doesn't need to keep living this life." His father picked up his rope again and yanked a strand through.

"And how was that Cara's fault?"

"She's just like her mother. Coming into our lives. Trying to convince you to stop working. Changing things in my life."

Nicholas stared at his father, feeling as if pieces of a puzzle were slowly falling into place. His father knew how Cara felt about Nicholas's jobs.

His mind ticked back to the last time he had talked to his father about cutting back on his hours on the job. The note of panic in his father's voice. How his father insisted Nicholas stick to the plan.

"We can't afford you quittin'," his father now said.

Nicholas leaned against the shed, the wood warm on his back. As he watched his father's quick, jerky movements, things that Cara said slipped into his mind.

Was he really enabling his father? Was he

really making it easy for his father to indulge in his hobbies while Nicholas was working?

The thought seemed disloyal, yet…

"Cara grew up with a lot of stuff," his father said after a moment of silence. "She's used to a higher standard of living than this ranch can give her."

"I don't think money is important to her, Dad," Nicholas said. "She told me she'd sooner have had her mother than the money Lori and Alan spent on her."

His father didn't answer and as Nicholas watched him, another thought spiraled up through his consciousness.

"Did Mom leave because money was tight?" he asked, giving voice to those thoughts. "Or was something else going on?"

His father stared down at the rope he'd been working on. "What do you mean?"

"You spent a lot of time at rodeos, didn't you?"

"You have to if you want to get to the qualifying rounds." Dale looked up at him, his eyes narrowed. "And if you're going to go on about the money it cost, like your mother always did, you know I often broke even."

"But was it really the money she was worried

about, Dad? Do you think she might have sooner had you around every weekend?"

Dale snorted his response, threw the rope down and surged to his feet. "Your mother would have been fine with everything if that Audra had stayed away from her. Your mom wanted more… and I couldn't give her what she wanted."

He stormed out of the shed, slamming the door so hard it banged shut and flew open again.

As it swung and creaked on its hinges, Nicholas bent over and picked up the rope, fingering the unwoven ends. He sighed as he hung it back up.

He had hit a sore spot with his questions to his father and for the first time in years, other speculations about his mother's leaving colored his thoughts.

And, as always, his mind drifted back to Cara and what she had said. How she had challenged him. She knew he loved working on the ranch. She knew what it meant.

He wasn't sure what was happening between them, but he wanted to see where it would go.

Talking to his father about her was a waste of time and breath. One of these days Dale would simply have to accept her as his…what?

Nicholas didn't want to think that far. Didn't dare. For now, he and Cara were together. For now they enjoyed being with each other. It felt right. Good. And it made his heart feel whole.

As for his father?

That he would have to deal with another time.

Chapter Fifteen

The corral was filled to bursting with cows, calves and heifers.

"Can't see why we need to test the whole works." Dale Chapman underlined his complaint with a frown.

"Just a precaution," Cara said, though she also didn't know why they were doing all the cattle. Nicholas was only shipping the thirty heifers across the border, and as far as she knew they were the only animals the buyer wanted tested for tuberculosis.

"Typical vet. Make you do more work than needs to be done." Dale glanced at her, his frown deepening. "I thought just Gordon, that new vet, was coming."

"He wanted some help." Cara kept her tone even as she climbed up and over the fence and away from Dale. She zeroed in on Nicholas, as if to draw strength from his presence. But he was talking to Dr. Moen.

When Gordon had asked her to come, her feelings were mixed. One part of her hoped to see Nicholas again. To test the change in their relationship.

Things were so tentative between them, so fragile, yet a sense of anticipation floated up within her. A sense of settling, which was both new and frightening.

She wasn't sure where this was going and she didn't know what kind of plans to make. But in the next week and a half she had to make a decision.

The job on which she had pinned so much of her hopes still waited. Yet to make a major life decision based on a few kisses and a few moments with Nicholas seemed foolish.

"You don't belong in a lab. You belong out here, working with animals."

Nicholas's comment twisted through her thoughts, shifting the foundations of her plans.

And then, there he was, standing in front of her, a gentle smile hovering around the edges of his mouth.

"I'm glad you could come out, too," Nicholas said, his voice igniting the spark of possibilities within her. "I was going to call you. See if you're free this weekend. I know you're on call all week."

"I'm not on call over the weekend."

"Great. What do you say to dinner in Calgary?"

Cara's smile started inside her and spread outward. The last time they spoke, Nicholas was leaving for Kuwait on the same day he wanted to go out with her.

"That sounds like a fabulous idea."

"Lorne told me about this restaurant. He said it would change my life."

"That's putting a lot of pressure on one restaurant." The unspoken message hovered between them and Cara's heart thudded heavily in her chest. Their eyes held as the import of his offer registered on both of them.

"No. There's no pressure at all." Nicholas's own smile grew as he reached out and feathered a strand of hair back from her face. "It's a bit fancy—"

"So no blue coveralls?" Cara asked, looking down at her own coveralls and trying to hide the flush in her cheeks, the sparkle of anticipation in her eyes.

"I'll take you exactly as you are," Nicholas said, his hand lingering on her cheek.

Cara looked up at that and as their eyes held, older, deeper emotions kindled and grew.

And with them a sense of coming home.

"I'm glad you came," Nicholas said, his hand drifting down to her shoulder. "I feel better knowing you're on the job, as well."

Cara caught Dale glancing at her, his eyes dark. Even from here his fury was as palpable as a slap.

She wished it didn't bother her. Wished he wasn't a shadow hanging over their growing relationship. But he was. And sooner or later, she and Nicholas would have to deal with Dale's feelings toward her.

"I think Gordon knows what he's doing," Cara said, shaking her head as if to turn her focus on the waiting job. "Besides, this is just a formality. Alberta is a TB-free zone."

"How long before we know anything?" Nicholas removed his hand, his voice growing businesslike.

"Two days."

"And then?"

"Then you'll be able to ship the cows and collect your paycheck." Cara added a grin to her comment, to show Nicholas she was kidding.

He didn't smile in return and Cara wondered if her comment about money bothered him.

"Gordon said he wanted to run the heifers through first so I better get them moved." Nicholas slipped on his gloves and jogged over to the corral without a backward glance as Cara regretted her ill-timed comment.

Though they had made plans for the weekend, he hadn't said anything about the job waiting for him in Kuwait and she hadn't said anything about her job in Montreal. It was as if they lived in a bubble, holding off reality.

But what would they do when reality intruded?

Cara looked around, taking in the scenery that was both peaceful and overwhelming. She tried to imagine staying here, becoming a part of the history permeating the house, the farm, the land.

She thought of Nicholas and how things had changed between them.

She had thought she and Nicholas had been in love the first time, but now, it seemed as if the feelings growing between them were different. Deeper. Richer.

And yes, it did make her afraid. Because she knew, this time around, if things didn't work out she would be more than hurt.

She would be devastated.

"This is an amazing place," Gordon said, turning around as if to get a better look. "These guys must be loaded to be able to afford to live here and keep it looking so good."

Cara glanced around the yard. Yes, it was

tidy, but Cara knew the sacrifices that had made it so.

"Nicholas works very hard," she said, unable to keep the defensive tone out of her voice.

"He must. From what I heard, all Dale does is hang around the auction mart. I saw him there both times I went with Bill."

"Hey, let's get these animals through," Dale called out from the corrals. "Haven't got all day."

Gordon raised his eyebrows and Cara made a note to talk to her uncle about the clinic's new vet. Gordon needed to learn a bit more discretion if he wanted to work in a close-knit farming community.

A cloud of dust from the milling cattle greeted them and a few minutes later they were immersed in the work.

Gordon called out the tag numbers of the cattle as he ran them through and Cara filled them in on the form.

Cara couldn't help feeling a burst of pride for Nicholas when she saw the heifers going through. They looked sleek and healthy, with beautiful conformation. They were some of the best cattle she'd ever seen and they would definitely improve the genetics of any herd they went to. Nicholas was a born rancher, she thought.

An hour and a half later the heifers were out

in the pasture again and the cloud of dust was settling in the corrals.

"So what's the next step?" Nicholas asked, pulling his hat off. He slapped it against his leg, beating the dust out.

Cara was about to speak when Gordon jumped in. "I have to come back and check the sites to see if there's been any reaction to the TB test."

"Still can't figure out why that loser wanted us to do a TB test," Dale grumbled. "Waste of time and money."

"He's the buyer and if that's what the buyer wants, that's what the buyer gets," Nicholas said. "It's just a precaution."

"You probably won't have to do this for the next group of cows you ship out," Cara assured Dale.

Dale nodded but didn't look at her, and apprehension shivered through her. Though she didn't need his approval, Dale's attitude would need to be dealt with if she and Nicholas's relationship were to deepen.

If.

The word hung over their relationship and Cara couldn't delve too deeply into it. Not yet.

"I'll only need to check a couple of the heifers," Gordon was saying as he walked with Nicholas toward the corrals. "Did you bring the other cows in, as well?"

"Because I'm not shipping them, I moved them out to the far pasture again. Besides, you said this test was a formality." Nicholas settled his hat lower on his head as the morning sun blinded him. Another beautiful day on the ranch.

"I did."

Nicholas climbed up and over a fence into the pen holding the heifers, the animals that represented the future.

Last night he had taken his horse out for a midnight ride as if hunting for some sign, some indication of what he should do. He knew his feelings for Cara were growing deeper every day and he knew he wanted to be with her.

But he also knew that she still wanted him to stay home. To work the ranch.

He'd imagined the picture and it tantalized. He thought of not having to take on work that required living in a guarded compound, watching your back while you made hard decisions about drilling, work conditions, employee discontent.

He wondered what it would be like to experience every day of every season on the ranch he loved so much.

He walked slowly through the milling heifers, glancing at their ear tags, easily recalling each of their mothers. He had chosen each of these heifers because their births had been problem free. Not that he would have known. He had been working on a rig in Newfoundland. His father was the one who'd been home to watch the births and make the necessary notations.

By being gone, he'd missed things happening on the ranch. Missed out on some of the rewards of the hard work.

And with that in mind, he'd worked up enough nerve to call his boss this morning. To talk about maybe cutting back on his hours. Maybe even quit completely. But he only got the answering machine.

He hadn't told Cara his plans. He wanted to surprise her when they went out for dinner.

Nor had he told his father.

However, sooner or later his father would have to accept that he and Cara were together again.

He pushed the thoughts aside as he focused on the work at hand. Clambering up on his horse, he clucked to it, then easily separated the first five heifers into the sorting pen and from there into the chute where Gordon could check them.

He got off his horse, closed the gate behind the first five and leaned on it while he watched Gordon move from animal to animal, checking the sites where they had done the TB test.

"Could you send another five in?" Gordon said, sounding distracted.

"Sure." Nicholas felt a niggle of unease. Cara and Gordon had both assured him this follow-up was simply a formality.

But he sorted five more out and sent them through.

When Gordon asked for five more, then another five, Nicholas's unease grew. They processed the entire herd and when he closed the gate on the last of the heifers, he rode his horse out through the gate and toward the other side of the chute.

Gordon checked the last five heifers, then nodded for Nicholas's father to open the head gate. The steel gate clanged and the heifers bawled as they charged to freedom, kicking up dust as Gordon pulled himself up and over the fence.

"What's wrong?" Nicholas asked. "Why did you need to check them all?"

Gordon wasn't looking at Nicholas as he pulled his gloves off. "I found three positives in the herd."

A roaring began in Nicholas's ears. "What do you mean?"

Gordon stuffed the gloves in his coverall pockets. "Sorry, Nick. Your herd has TB."

The roaring grew. "I thought Alberta was TB free. Where could it have come from?"

"Possibly some of the semen you used when you artificially inseminated your cattle."

"So what does this mean?"

Gordon glanced over his shoulder at the shining, fat, healthy-looking animals. The cream of Nicholas's herd.

"Quarantine." The word came out like a bullet and Nicholas grabbed one of the uprights on the corrals to steady himself.

Quarantine.

A word associated with diseases that killed animals and livelihoods. Quarantine was the first step to something far more serious. "And after that?"

Gordon gave a listless shrug as if his diagnosis was simply another day on the job and didn't mean the destruction of a herd Nicholas had spent years building up. "All the animals on this farm will have to be destroyed."

"Horses, too?"

"Not sure about them, but my guess would be yeah." Gordon peeled his coveralls off, stepped out of them and bunched them up. As if he was going to dispose of them as soon as he got back to the clinic.

"So what do we do?" Nicholas couldn't stop the note of desperation in his voice. He couldn't imagine the herd had to be wiped out because of one random test. "Could you test them again? Is there something we can do?"

"Not a thing to do." Gordon shoved the

coveralls under his arm. "I have a bunch of paperwork to work through and then I have to make the call. Meantime, none of your animals goes anywhere."

The cattle liner was coming tomorrow to pick up the herd.

He already had half of the buyer's money in the farm account, and most of that was already earmarked for special projects. The rest was supposed to have been their living money until he sold the crop.

Now he had to give it all back. And he was looking at the destruction of years of work. Gone.

Cara parked her car by the barn and got out. As soon as she heard the news from Gordon, she cancelled her next appointments, jumped in the car and came straight to the Chapman ranch.

She heard the bawling of animals and ran to the corrals where she hoped the heifers were still penned up. Awaiting orders from Gordon.

When Gordon told her what he'd found, she could hardly believe it. There hadn't been a case of TB in cattle in Alberta for years. And these animals had no genetic connection to any herds in Canada or the States proven to carry tuberculosis.

She knew it was unprofessional of her, but she

needed to see for herself and double-check Gordon's diagnosis.

As she came around the corner, her gaze scanned the corrals looking for Nicholas, but she only saw Dale, standing with his hands in his pockets, staring over the penned-up heifers.

Cara hesitated but then walked over to his side.

"I'm so sorry, Dale," she said.

He didn't look at her, but kept his eyes on the seemingly healthy herd. "I can't believe we have to kill them all. They're the best animals we've ever raised."

"I can't believe it either," she said quietly. She hesitated to ask the next question, but she had to for Nicholas's sake. "Would you mind if I checked them myself?"

Dale gave a short laugh. "Go crazy. Won't do any harm."

Cara wasn't sure what to think of that comment, but she climbed over the fence anyhow. The animals turned to look at her, which made it difficult to see the test sites for herself. But a few kept their backs turned to her and when one swished its tail, she saw the telltale swelling.

It wasn't quite as significant as she thought it should be. Not according to what she'd seen in her textbooks or the pictures she'd checked online before she came.

But it was a reaction and she knew they couldn't ignore it.

The animals jostled each other as they moved around in reaction to her presence. They looked so sleek and healthy. Their eyes were clear and they didn't so much as sniffle.

Cara stood, her hands on her hips, watching the cattle, a sense of something off-kilter niggling at her. But she couldn't grab hold of it or formulate it. Western Canada had been TB free for years. She knew Nicholas and his father had handpicked these animals from their own herd. They had used artificial insemination to improve the genetics.

Why here and why now in this herd?

The thought of these healthy-looking animals being slaughtered created a dull ache in her chest. What a waste.

Surely something wasn't right?

She climbed over the fence, scaring a flock of sparrows drinking from the cattle waterer. Her heart jumped as they exploded up into the sky.

"Told Nicholas he should shoot those things," Dale mumbled as Cara's heart settled. "They've been hanging around the waterer steady the past couple of weeks. Found a bunch of dead ones in the barn."

"Where is Nicholas?" Cara asked.

Dale scratched his forehead with his forefinger. "Packing for Calgary."

"Why Calgary?" And why now? They had a crisis on their hands.

"He's going back to work."

Cara stared at him as the words beat in her mind in time with the flapping of the sparrows' wings overhead. Of course. Nicholas's solution to the problem.

Then she turned and strode to the house, her hands curled into fists, her feat pounding out a hard rhythm.

Had everything he said to her been a lie? His talk about staying, about taking a chance, about putting down roots, about hating the restlessness of his life? Was it all just so he could steal a few kisses?

Steal her heart again?

She stormed up the walk just as Nicholas appeared in the doorway, a duffel bag slung over one shoulder, a suitcase in his other hand.

As soon as he saw her, he dropped both to the porch with a resounding thunk. His eyes skimmed past her, looking somewhere over her shoulder.

"So what's going on?" she asked.

"I'm leaving for Calgary tonight. I have a meeting and I'm flying out tomorrow. I was going to come over before I left."

"To kiss me goodbye?"

"Cara, I'm so sorry, but I don't have any choice."

"And us? What about us?"

Nicholas frowned. "I'm only gone for two months. I'll be back."

"How are we supposed to maintain a relationship when you're halfway across the world?"

"We can e-mail. Phone. Internet calls. It's not that hard to maintain a long-distance relationship these days."

"I don't want a long-distance relationship. I want you."

The words flew out of her mouth before she could stop them. Great. Now she sounded like some pathetic whiner who couldn't live without her boyfriend for a couple of months.

"I have to go, Cara," was all he said, regret tingeing his voice.

"Why?"

Nicholas shoved his hand through his hair, then turned to her, and when Cara saw helplessness and fear in his eyes, her resolve wavered.

"You know what Gordon said. The heifers—they'll be destroyed. Tomorrow Dad is rounding up the rest of the cows from the far pastures and bringing them down here. They're going to be killed, too."

Cara easily heard the pain in his voice and

knew how dearly this would cost him. Would cost the ranch. But was leaving the only solution?

"I could ask Gordon to do another test, to try again—"

"I talked to Gordon. He's already put in the order to slaughter the herd."

"I can't believe every problem has to be solved by you, or by you working away from the ranch. Isn't there anything else you can do?"

Nicholas turned to her and she caught a flash of despair in his eyes. "What? Carpentry work? Driving a school bus? Maybe working part-time at the Seed and Feed in Cochrane? Or how about I work at the auction mart for about nine dollars an hour? And maybe, after ten years of that, I'll be able to build up my herd again and support a family." He sliced the air with his hand. "Truth is, Cara, I make more in one tour on the rigs than I would in four years of working at any other job."

"So the money is that important to you?"

"You say it isn't to you, but that changes over time."

"I don't want you to go, Nicholas," she said.

Nicholas reached out to her, as if to help her understand. "Don't ask me to stay. Please don't make me choose again."

Cara pressed her hand against her chest as if

to push down her rising fear and with that, her anger. He still didn't get it.

"If you leave again, Nicholas, we're right back to where we were three years ago. I'm not going there. I thought we were through that, I thought we had both grown and changed, but it looks like you haven't at all."

Nicholas stared at her. "And have you? You accuse me of running off, but are you still leaving for Montreal?"

"I wasn't going to."

"Wasn't?" A frown creased his forehead as he zeroed in on that vague word.

"No. I wasn't. But you leave me no choice."

"Cara—"

She held up her hand to block his protest, to put up a shield against his heartrending appeal. "Your job is too dangerous."

"I always come back, Cara."

His words snaked into her mind, an eerie echo of her mother's.

She glanced down at the leg he had broken the last time. She remembered the stories she'd heard of threats on workers' lives, thinking of the casual way his coworker had talked about kidnappings and ransoms.

And as she turned her eyes back to him her past came crashing into her present and her throat thickened with old pain and old sorrow. "That's exactly what my mother always said."

"What do you mean?"

Cara wrapped her arms around herself, as if to contain the sorrow that she had walled in these past few years.

But Nicholas's gentle foray into her heart had softened her. Had made her vulnerable and the pain sifted too easily through the breaks he had created in her fortifications.

"Every time she left she told me the work wasn't dangerous. And when I pleaded with her to stay, not to leave me alone, she told me not to be selfish. Not to think of myself. That her work was important and that she would be back." Cara couldn't stop the hitch in her voice. "And then one time she didn't come back. And I was alone." She swallowed and swallowed, struggling to maintain her composure as the pain she had held back so long came crashing back.

She looked up at Nicholas, at the face that had grown so dear to her. At the eyes that could melt her heart with one look. At the mouth that promised so much and the arms that gave her security and shelter.

She couldn't stay behind, waiting each time he left, wondering, as she had with her mother, if he would return.

"It took that one time to tear my world apart,"

she cried, her hands clutching her sides. "And I'm not going through that again. I can't, Nicholas. I can't live with that fear hanging over my head each time you leave. I can't think of losing you." She dashed the tears away, not caring that he saw her like this, not caring that she had lost control of her emotions.

Nicholas stared at her, as if finally realizing what his leaving might cost her.

"Cara, please—"

"Stop. I know the ranch is important and I know how much you've put into it, but if you leave I can't stay and put myself through that pain again."

She waited a moment, as if her declaration might change something, anything between them, but he made no move toward her, said nothing to change her mind.

Then she turned, stumbled down the steps and ran toward her car.

Every step she took away from Nicholas was like a shot to her own heart.

She knew she would never see him again.

Chapter Sixteen

"Can't sleep, honey?" Aunt Lori walked into the half-darkened living room and settled herself on the couch beside Cara as the grandfather clock in the corner rang two o'clock in the morning. "What are you reading?"

"The Psalms. Trying to find out what I'm supposed to learn through all of this." Cara's eyes were dry. She had cried all the way back from Nicholas's place, praying that she wouldn't get into an accident. Thankfully neither Uncle Alan nor Aunt Lori was home when she got here.

She had hidden herself away in her bedroom, letting the tears flow until her eyes burned.

After supper she had gone back to her bedroom but sleep had eluded her.

She'd been here for four hours already, reading, praying—anything to keep from looking into the bleak and cheerless landscape of her future.

Cara turned another page. "I thought Nicholas and I were on our way to a new and better place. I even thought, in one silly, hopeful corner of my mind, that he would propose again."

Aunt Lori slipped her arm around her niece's shoulder. "I'm so sorry, honey. I was starting to see such hope and joy in your eyes. I was starting to make my own silly plans." She squeezed Cara, offering what comfort she could. "Have you called Mr. Rousseau in Montreal?"

"He's not in the office until tomorrow. I was going to call him then and let him know I wasn't coming."

"And now?"

The words hung between them.

"I'm taking the job," Cara said finally. "It's a great opportunity. And it will take me halfway across the country."

"And away from Nicholas."

Cara didn't reply.

Aunt Lori sighed and stroked Cara's head. "I'm sure you know what you're doing. I wish there was a way to solve Nicholas's problem with the cattle. Because if that happened, maybe he wouldn't leave."

"Am I being selfish because I don't want Nicholas to work those risky jobs? I know he wants to save his ranch but if this is Nicholas's way of solving all his money problems that won't change in the future. There will always be something to fix, repair or buy."

Aunt Lori gave her a reassuring smile. "No, honey. You're not selfish. I think Nicholas feels he has no choice, which, of course, is never true. We all have a choice and it's how we make our choices that determine what is most important in our lives."

"And for him, it's the ranch. Always will be the ranch. How can I compete with that?"

"You don't have to fight the ranch or compete with it. Maybe you just have to embrace it, understand it. I know you've been looking for community and roots, but I also think you've been afraid to get too settled."

"What do you mean?"

Aunt Lori angled her head to one side as if to look at the problem from another viewpoint. "I remember telling your mother it wasn't fair to you, to move you around from place to place, and that she had to do something about it. For your sake."

"Is that why she left me here?"

"One of the reasons." Aunt Lori picked up Cara's hand and gently stroked it with her thumb. "She said something to me once that didn't sink in until recently. How she was afraid of you."

"Afraid?" What could Aunt Lori be talking about? "My mother wasn't afraid of anything."

Aunt Lori's gentle look held a shadow of pity as she squeezed Cara's hand. "I think she was afraid of getting too attached to you. You never knew your father, and though he was never in your life, your mother cared for him a lot more than she let on. When he died, it sent her into a tailspin of grief. I think she always hoped he would come to his senses and come back to her and you. And I think her reaction to his death was to throw herself into whatever work she could to get rid of the grief."

"She always told me I was lucky to be born where I was, and that she had to help these other children." Cara's heart seemed to fold in on itself, as if protecting itself once again from the pain of the past. "It was like she always chose them over me."

"That was her way of keeping you at arm's length." Aunt Lori's voice was suddenly quiet and steady. "I tried to tell her she would be the one who would lose in the end. Trouble was you were the one that lost the most. I think you lost the ability to give yourself completely to anyone because you were afraid that whatever you love might get taken away."

The tiniest crack tremored through Cara's defenses. "When I asked Nicholas not to go, I felt like I was a little girl again. Asking my mother not to go." Cara sighed. "Do you think I'm afraid of loving Nicholas, too?"

"What do you think?"

Aunt Lori's simple question placed doubt on Cara's arguments against loving Nicholas. The arguments she built to defend her heart. Then she released a heavy sigh. "Maybe."

"Do you think he loves you?"

"I don't know. If he does, why would he leave?"

Aunt Lori released Cara's hand and sat back, folding her arms around her middle, as if trying to find the best way to answer.

"When your uncle had his heart attack, I resented every minute he'd spent at the clinic. I thought if only he hadn't worked so hard he would have been fine. And maybe that was true. But I also know that your uncle defines himself through work. For Alan a large part of his significance is not only in his work, but also in being able to provide for the people he loves. I think Nicholas is of a similar character and if you care for Nicholas, you need to appreciate the things he appreciates."

"I know what the ranch means to him. I didn't get that the first time."

"Then you'll have to understand why he does what he does."

"So you're saying Nicholas is right to head off?"

Aunt Lori responded with a shrug. "I'm not saying he's right or wrong. I'm just saying that if you care about him, you'll realize his dedication to the ranch is a vital part of who he is."

"And what about me? Where do I fit in this?"

Aunt Lori's only response was a careful lift of one eyebrow encouraging Cara to explain.

"I have to protect…protect myself," she continued, pleading with her aunt to understand her stumbling answers. "It's the only way I'll survive."

"Survive?"

Cara's resolve weakened with each question her aunt lobbed her way.

"Yes. Survive." A throb of an older emotion passed through her, as the pain she had exposed to Nicholas returned.

"That makes it sound like you're on your own. Like you have to get through life on your own strength." Though Aunt Lori's words were gently spoken they held the gentlest lash of reprimand.

Ashamed, Cara looked down at the Bible in her lap and her gaze was caught by the word *strength*. She read the passage aloud. "'Blessed are those whose strength is in You.'"

"Those words are true for all of us," Aunt Lori said. "Me as well as you. I know I had to cling to that when Uncle Alan was in the hospital, and I still have to realize my strength and my trust is in God, not myself."

Cara ran her finger along the edge of the page, drawing up the old memories she had thrown at Nicholas. "When mom died, I had to think of what she always told me. That you have to take care of yourself."

"She was wrong, Cara. Taking care of yourself turns you into an island. Thinking only of yourself pushes other people and their needs away. You're a better person than that. You have a good heart. Please don't take on your mother's problems." Aunt Lori released a light sigh as she stroked Cara's hair. "When she died, I wanted nothing more than to hold you close, to let you know we were here, but you were older, so independent. So much, in some ways, like your mother. So I kept my distance, waiting for you to let me know how you felt. Waiting to hear from your own mouth how much it hurt. But you kept us at a distance."

Cara covered her mouth with her hand, holding back the trembling. "I'm sorry, Aunty. I felt so alone. And I pushed you away and I pushed God away. I was doing exactly what my mother told me to do. Taking care of myself." Cara turned to her aunt. "Just like I did the last time I left. The last time Nicholas and I fought. I'm sorry I didn't call as often as I should have. I'm sorry that I kept myself separate from you. I thought if I did, I wouldn't hurt as much."

"Did it work?"

Cara shook her head as hot tears welled up. "I missed you so much."

Aunt Lori gently brushed an errant tear from Cara's cheek. "I know you did. But I'm also guessing you missed Nicholas."

Cara sighed. "I did. Horribly."

"And you will again. I know losing your mother made you afraid, but how would you sooner live? Alone? Safe? Or would you sooner risk loving someone? When you left I was so hurt. And I'm not telling this to make you feel guilty, just to explain. I could have avoided that hurt by not taking you in at all. Your uncle and I could have kept our lives free and uncluttered." Aunt Lori's expression softened and she reached out and tucked a strand of hair behind Cara's ear. "But we would have missed out on all the good things we had having you in our home. Love causes pain and makes you vulnerable to pain, but it's worth every hurt for the blessing it gives you."

Cara couldn't say anything. She bent her head and let her aunt's words wear away the walls around her heart.

"And I hope you also realize that God loves you in spite of how you feel about Him," Aunt Lori continued. "That though we hurt Him over and over, and I include myself, your uncle and every person in this world when I say that, His love is unconditional and enduring."

Her aunt's words ignited a new sorrow. She had been so wrong to push her aunt and uncle away. To push God away.

To keep Nicholas at arm's length, blaming his work, his choices.

Tears thickened her throat. Tears of regret. Sorrow.

But this sorrow had a cleansing quality. And as she laid her head on her aunt's shoulder, she felt surrounded not just by her aunt's arms, but also by the love of God. A God who knew her before she was born. Who hemmed her in behind and before.

When the sorrow abated, she lifted her head again. The pain was still there, but now she had a companion, a support in the darkness.

She was about to close the Bible when a phrase caught her attention.

She stopped and read it again.

My heart and flesh cry out for the living God. Even the sparrow has found a home.

Something niggled at her, but she couldn't seem to catch it and pin it down.

Aunt Lori stroked her niece's cheek, stifling a yawn. "I'm sorry, my dear, but I have to go to bed." She laid her hand on Cara's shoulder. "Are you going to be okay?"

Cara nodded. "I'm staying up for a bit. Read some more."

"I'll be praying as you make your decisions." Aunt Lori cupped her chin, then dropped a light kiss on her head. "And you know that no matter what you decide, no matter where you go, your uncle and I will always love you and this will always be your home."

As she left, her aunt's words kindled warmth and yearning in Cara.

Home.

She glanced around the familiar setting of the living room as echoes of conversations held here, memories of family games and times spent reading, hovered in the quiet.

A few memories of living with her mother slipped in, as well, but they were less clear. She had no memory whatsoever of a grandmother and nothing to remember her by.

She thought of Nicholas, and of the antiques that had been handled by his grandparents and great-grandparents. They were no mere artifacts. They were part of his history and had stories attached to them. Stories woven into the fabric of his life and rooted in his history.

And she knew despite her anger and hurt, she still cared for Nicholas and because the caring was so strong, the hurt at his choice was so great.

Was he really choosing the ranch over you?

She shook her head as if to dislodge her doubts, but other thoughts returned. Memories of the pride in Nicholas's voice as he pointed out the places on his ranch that meant so much. Places that had history and stories. Nicholas was rooted and grounded in that place. It wasn't competition for her, it was a part of who he was. And if she were honest with herself, she would realize that if she loved him, then she had to love what made him who he was.

She felt a moment of freedom at that thought and she looked down at the Bible again. She hadn't turned the page.

Even the sparrow...

As it had before, the single word caught her attention.

Sparrow. Sparrows flying around the barn. Sparrows clustered around a waterer. Sparrows dead on the ground.

And she had a good idea of what had happened with Nicholas's cattle.

The view from the hotel was amazing. At least according to the project manager who put him up here after their meeting last night. The beds were purported to be the most comfortable in the city, guaranteeing him the best night's sleep.

But Nicholas had spent most of the night clutching his cell phone, second thoughts bouncing around his skull.

Was he doing the right thing?

Should he phone Cara? Talk things over with her?

And what could he say that hadn't been said on the porch? Things between him and Cara had been coming together. And his feelings for her were stronger than before. Deeper.

But what choice did he have? Losing the cattle meant losing income he did not know how else to replace. The ranch couldn't absorb that kind of loss. And there was no way he was going to make a commitment to Cara unless he knew for sure he could provide for her.

He'd finally fallen into busy dreams around two o'clock and had woken up an hour ago.

An airplane soared past his window and beyond that the Rocky Mountains thrust rugged peaks into a sky pink from the sunrise.

Below him, he could see the suburbs of north Calgary. A maze of houses and streets flowing over the hills and leading to the mountains. In another hour people would be leaving home for work for the day and returning at night to their families.

In half an hour he had to leave for the airport, cram himself into a seat meant for someone four inches shorter and look forward to twenty-five hours of flights and stopovers. And after that?

Twelve-hour workdays. Evenings spent watching television with men who were also far away from their homes.

He leaned his head against the window. He was already missing Cara.

What am I supposed to do, Lord? How can I find my way through this?

Going out to do this work was the only way he could guarantee the ranch could provide for his family. For Cara.

I have learned the secret of being content in any and every situation, whether well fed or hungry, whether living in plenty or in want.

The words from Philippians that he had spoken so blithely to his father seemed to taunt him.

But that was before he found out his cattle herd and his plans for a future living on the ranch with Cara were wiped out with one visit from the vet.

Do they have to be?

Nicholas pushed himself away from the window, and grabbed his suitcase. He'd already told his boss he was leaving. Had the plane ticket in his pocket. He was committed.

And what of your commitment to Cara?

He paused, his hands wrapped around the handle as indecision dogged his every move.

He looked out the window again. The sun was above the mountains, bathing the city in a pinkish glow. Once the heifers were shipped out, he had hoped to take Cara out early one morning and show her the sun coming up over the ranch.

He'd imagined himself standing behind her, his arms wrapped around her, holding her close. Then he'd imagined himself asking her, quietly, if she'd consider making their relationship more serious. If she would consider a future with him.

And you walked out on that?

What else was he supposed to do? Stay around and watch his herd of cattle being destroyed? His plans for the future?

I have learned the secret of being content in every situation…I can do everything through Him who gives me strength.

Nicholas let go of the suitcase and dropped on the bed behind him. So if he went and made his money, he'd have his ranch.

But he wouldn't have Cara.

He tried to imagine his life without her. He'd done it before, but he knew, this time, losing her would not just break his heart, it would destroy it.

Lorne had told him love was a risk.

Maybe he didn't dare take that risk with Cara the first time. Maybe the first time, when he chose his work over her, maybe it wasn't just about the work. Maybe, deep down, it was also about the risk of loving someone who could potentially break his heart.

Who could potentially leave.

So, simple answer to that, be the first to leave.

A chill surrounded his heart, the same heart he had unwittingly protected as the words took root. And he knew this was the biggest part of his struggle.

I can do everything through Him who gives me strength.

He had treated Cara badly. She was right to be concerned that he had chosen the ranch over her.

And behind that thought came a more chilling one.

He was just like her mother.

Just like his mother.

He lowered his head into his hands as he struggled to let go of the thoughts, the concerns, the worries.

Forgive me, Lord. Forgive my need to be in

charge. To be in control. Forgive me for not put-ting You first in my life and for not making Cara a priority. Help me to serve You, Lord. Help me to lean on You for wisdom and for strength. Show me what I should do.

He waited a moment, as if for an answer, but as the silence of his hotel room filled his ears, a conviction grew deep within him.

And accompanying that, a sense of release.

He wanted Cara in his life. And he wanted to stay on the ranch regardless of what might come. To build a life with her there. Every day. And he had to trust and believe that she meant every word when she said money didn't matter. That she would sooner have him around every day than a financially secure ranch.

Please, Lord. Give me the strength to follow through on this.

He waited a moment, then added:

Please let Cara still be there.

Chapter Seventeen

"I think it's worth a shot. You've got nothing to lose." Cara stood in front of Dale Chapman, stifling her frustration with the man.

"Except my time," Dale growled back.

Cara shot him an exasperated frown. This morning she had gone directly to the vet clinic with her new information, hoping to convince Gordon to hold off on the order to destroy the cattle. He hadn't budged.

Now she faced the same unyielding behavior from the man who had the most to gain from her coming here.

"I thought you wanted to save the cows."

"How do you figure you know more than that Gordon fella? He's been a vet longer than you have."

And been moving from clinic to clinic ever since he'd received his license, Cara found out.

"Because he doesn't care. He's here because he can't get work anywhere else. It doesn't matter to him that the entire herd you and your son have spent years building up could be destroyed with one stroke of his pen."

"And you do care?" Dale challenged.

"I care a lot more than he does. I don't want to see the ranch lose any more money."

"Nicholas isn't here, you know."

"I know. But I still want to do this for him."

"I still think it's a waste of time."

Cara finally couldn't stand this anymore. "Your son is heading out to a dangerous job so he can save this ranch. He's willing to put his life on the line for this place and you can't put aside your own stubborn pride or your unreasonable dislike of me to let me run one single, simple, lousy test?"

Dale looked taken aback at her anger, but she wasn't near done.

"How dare you act as if I don't know what I'm doing?" Cara's voice grew quiet. "From the first moment you met me you've judged me and made me feel like I don't deserve your son. Let me set one thing straight, my uncle feels the same way about him. Neither of us deserves the other but I know that in Christ, he and I are equal and you and I are equal. I don't know what I've ever done to make you dislike—"

"How about leaving my son? Just like his mother left me and him?"

"You disliked me even before we broke up so don't use that excuse," Cara snapped. "And you're right. I shouldn't have left him. I should have stayed. But I had my own reasons and I don't think they were wrong."

"This ranch is important to him, missy. You have to know that."

"Do you think I don't?" Cara's voice grew more intense. "I've seen how the light shines in his eyes when he looks around this place. I know how his voice gets soft whenever he talks about it. I know it's in his blood and his soul and I know he shouldn't have to leave it every time this place needs something fixed."

"His mother couldn't make the sacrifice to stay, what makes you think—"

"Don't even mention us in the same breath. I'm not like her." Cara's voice rose with each sentence and she didn't care anymore. Her anger was burning white-hot. "And if you think I can't make any sacrifices for Nicholas or for this ranch, you might want to talk to my supposed boss in Montreal, who I called this morning to tell him that I won't be coming on time because I want to do an acid-fast test on sparrow poop. And he told me not to bother coming at all, so technically, I don't have a job because I want to find a way to save Nicholas's cows."

She caught Dale looking past her and she was about to grab him to make him look at her when she caught the puzzled look on his face.

She turned and her heart stopped, then flopped slowly over.

Nicholas was striding toward them, his gaze intent on her.

"What you doing here, son?" Dale asked. "Aren't you supposed to be on a plane?"

Cara couldn't speak. She could only look at him, soaking in the reality of him standing in front of her.

"I changed my mind," Nicholas said, answering his father's questions but addressing Cara.

She continued to stare at him, unable to believe he was really here.

He took her hands in his. "I'm sorry," he said, his voice quiet, his eyes intent on hers.

She stood immobile, still struggling to believe he was here. Not winging across the Atlantic to a remote oil rig.

"Why did you come back?" she asked, her voice a breathless whisper taking in the strength of him. The very presence of him.

"I don't want to leave you alone again," he said, squeezing her hands tighter in return. "I want to stay here. With you."

Cara's breath left her in a sigh, then a tentative smile hovered at the corner of her mouth. "I'm glad you came back."

Then she gave into an impulse and reached up and cupped his jaw in her hand and, in front of his father, stood up on tiptoe and kissed him.

He swept her into his arms and kissed her back, holding her tight against him. She felt safe, secure.

Cared for.

"I'm so sorry," he murmured. "I was wrong."

"So was I," she whispered, her arms twining around his neck, her fingers tangling in his hair. She gave him another kiss, relishing the privilege.

She wished she could push the world away. Wished time could stop so she could stay here, absorbing the reality of his presence. Things still lay between them that she wanted swept away.

But reality intruded and she reluctantly pulled back.

"What are you doing here?" he asked, his finger tracing her features with a gentleness that almost melted her resolve.

She brushed a kiss over his knuckles, then reluctantly lowered his hand.

"I'm trying to convince your father to let me run some tests to prove the heifers are perfectly healthy."

Nicholas blinked, as if trying to catch up to her. "I thought there was nothing else you could do?"

"Your cows don't have bovine TB," she said, forcing her attention back to the matter at hand. For now it was enough that Nicholas was here to help her solve this problem and she needed him on board to convince his stubborn father. "But I'm pretty sure they have been exposed to avian TB, which is benign to most humans and cattle, but can show a false positive in a TB test. Gordon should have known that."

"So how..." Nicholas, still holding her hand, tried to sift this information.

"You've been holding the heifers close to the barn for the past couple of months. I'm convinced if we check the cows in the upper pasture you won't find any reaction to the TB test because they weren't exposed to the sparrows living in the barn."

"And how do you know those birds have whatever it is you think they have," Dale interrupted, his puzzled glance ticking from Nicholas to Cara as if trying to absorb this new situation.

Cara's frustration eased with Nicholas standing beside her. "A simple acid test on the sparrow droppings will confirm what I suspect. And the fact that they're showing some of the classic symptoms. When I saw the flock of birds at the waterer the other day, it raised a red flag." Which was only brought to her attention when she read the piece in the Psalms about the sparrow.

"Will that test be enough?" Nicholas asked.

"Alberta is classified as TB free. I know once I do the test and present this information to Uncle Alan and Bill, they'll corroborate my findings. We might have to do a follow-up test on the heifers, but they'll get a clean bill of health. The TB test wasn't even mandatory."

"But it caused a lot of problems."

"And the fact that your other herd won't show any reaction to the test will be proof, as well, that it isn't in the heifers," Cara continued, looking back to Nicholas.

Nicholas's smile dove into her heart and though a thousand questions still hung between them, the reality was he was standing beside her instead of sitting on a plane.

That was more then enough for now.

"Okay. Let's do this then. Tell us what we need to do and we'll do it."

Nicholas tried not to chew his lip, fidget or sigh. Cara had been busy making up slides in the vet clinic for the past half an hour. After she had come to the ranch, Nicholas and his father had ridden up to the other herd and brought them down to the corrals. Cara had gone through them all and had found no reaction to the test, which corroborated her diagnosis.

After that they had helped her gather up sparrow droppings from the barn and bagged a few dead sparrows, as well.

He still couldn't believe the sight that had greeted him when he came to the ranch from Calgary. Cara's car parked in the driveway.

Cara standing up to his father, arguing with him.

The look of surprise and pleasure when she saw him walking toward her.

He wanted to sweep her off her feet, whisk her away to a secluded place where they could talk, share and remove the debris of the last argument they'd had.

But that had to wait while she pushed another slide under the microscope, determined to prove her theory.

He couldn't read her expression at all. Her entire focus was on what she could see through the lens.

She took one slide off, and put yet another one underneath it and looked through it again.

Finally Alan spoke up.

"So? What did you see?" Uncle Alan pushed his glasses up his nose. Nicholas knew Alan needed to know the results as badly as he did. To have a positive TB test show up in Alberta cattle could be devastating for the local ranchers.

Finally Cara straightened, stretching her arms over her head. Then she gave Nicholas a grin that made him sag against the wall behind him.

"The sparrow droppings tested positive for avian TB," she said, her quiet words thundering in Nicholas's head.

"That's wonderful," Alan said.

Wonderful didn't begin to cover the relief surging through Nicholas. Though he had confidence in Cara, hearing her confirm her diagnosis pushed away the last doubt he had.

"I know a follow-up test on the heifers will show them to be clear, as well." She gave Nicholas another smile. "You won't be able to ship them until we do the next test, but in the meantime, everything is clear."

"Are you going to go by her word?" Gordon blustered from the doorway of the makeshift lab Cara had set up. "She doesn't have near the experience with hands-on vet work that I do. I should have been the one to check that other herd. It was my case."

Nicholas saw Alan shoot Gordon a withering look. Then, as if Gordon didn't matter, Alan turned to Nicholas. "I'm rescinding the order to destroy the herd."

Thank You, Lord, Nicholas thought. He didn't deserve the break, but he was thankful for it.

"But you can't go over my head—" Gordon was saying.

"I can and I will," Uncle Alan retorted.

"If you're taking her word over mine, I don't know if I can work in this office," Gordon said, his hands shoved into the pockets of his smock.

"You don't have to worry about thinking you can't work in this office. It will be a reality," Uncle Alan said in a clipped voice.

Nicholas glanced from Alan to Gordon, wondering what was going on.

Alan turned to Cara. "If you'll excuse me, I have to have a chat with Gordon and Bill." He patted her on the shoulder. "Good work, girl. I'm so proud of your dedication."

He left, closing the door quietly behind him, leaving Nicholas and Cara alone in the room.

As soon as the door clicked behind him, Nicholas spun Cara around on the chair and pulled her up into his arms.

Then he caught her mouth in a long, deep and satisfying kiss.

When he came up for air, her eyes shone up at him, and her hands clung to his shoulders.

"Okay," she said, her voice sounding shaky. "I guess we're not going to bother with words."

"They have traditionally come between us."

Nicholas turned and sat down on the stool and pulled her close. "But I do have something to say."

He waited, letting the silence settle to allow the moment its full due.

"I'm sorry. I'm so sorry," he said. "I was wrong. You were right."

"Please. No. I was wrong, too. Wrong not to see that the ranch wasn't competition. That it was a part of you—an important and vital part of you."

Nicholas shook his head, still trying to reconcile the fact that he was here, holding Cara in his arms.

"You know, you were right. It isn't all up to me. I was in a mad panic to head out to go and save the ranch when, in the end, you did it. You were the one who saved the ranch."

She put her finger to his lips. "No. It wasn't me. I had to learn to listen." Her voice was suddenly quiet and steady as if she needed him to understand. "I had to learn to let go and to not put myself first." She removed her finger and replaced it with another kiss. "I'm so thankful God brought us together again and I want you in my life and I'll take you as you are. Right now."

Though she spoke the words lightly, he knew their true cost.

And his heart thrilled with possibilities.

"Will you?"

"Will I what?"

"Will you take me as I am? Right now?" He couldn't stop himself, he had to know. "Would you marry me?"

Cara held his gaze, her smile creating an answering burst of pleasure inside him. "Yes. I will."

Nicholas bent his head and sealed their promises with a gentle, lingering kiss. Then he sighed. "This wasn't exactly where I had planned to propose," he said, thinking of the hillside, the sunset and having everything just right.

"This is as good a place as any." Cara glanced around the tiny room with its shelves of medicine and supplies. "You had everything perfect the first time around but that was no guarantee of success."

"Not toward the end." He gave a rueful laugh. "You sure you're willing to give engagement to me another go?"

"I think we're getting pretty good at it." Cara clasped her hands behind his neck, leaning back to look at him. "We're starting from another place."

"You're right about that. I'm not going to the rigs again," he said. "I want to stay on the ranch full-time, though I won't make as much money."

Her look held a vestige of sorrow. "Do you think that matters to me?"

"No. I suppose it wouldn't." He released a nervous laugh. "Not like it mattered to my mother. But like you suggested, I think she was lonely and being broke didn't help. And you, living with your aunt and uncle, always seemed to have more than enough. But I never realized what you had to live with."

"Doesn't matter. It all came together to bring me here. To meet you."

"Again," he said with a laugh.

"Again."

He kissed her again, then traced the line of her lips. "You know I love you, Cara Morrison."

"And I love you, Nicholas Chapman."

The words hung between them, rife with promises and hope. Hope for today and for a future.

"Let's go tell my uncle," Cara said, tugging on his arm. "I'm sure he's wondering what's going on in here."

"Oh, I think he has a pretty good idea," Nicholas said.

"And then we should go talk to your father."

Nicholas pulled her back. "I'm sorry about him, too," he went on, realizing it needed to be said. "I'm sure he'll come around in time."

Cara slanted him a half smile. "I guess I'll have to turn on the charm, then, won't I?"

"Or tell him he can get free vet services," Nicholas said.

"Maybe I'll have to start my own business," Cara said, pulling open the door. "Be competition to my uncle and Bill." She stepped out into the hallway, almost colliding with Gordon, who shot Cara a baleful glance before slamming the back door behind him.

Nicholas looked from the door, to Cara then to Alan standing in the doorway of his office, his hands on his hips.

"Something tells me you might have a job waiting right here," he said. He slipped his arm over her shoulders and in front of her uncle, dropped a kiss on her head, then together they walked toward him to share their good news.

Together.

* * * * *

Dear Reader,

This story came to me while I was doing research for another book. That often happens to writers. It's as if our internal radar is always searching. But the concept had to be put aside while other ideas clamored to be given form, so I was glad to finally tell Cara and Nicholas's story. What I was trying to show with this book is the false idea of thinking we have control over our lives. We can make all our plans and then, like Nicholas, things happen beyond our control and everything is in turmoil. I know I struggle again and again with thinking, again like Nicholas, that if everything is exactly right in my life, then I can be happy. Whereas, instead, I've had to learn to be content this moment with where I am. To look to God and realize that the most important plans I can make are with Him in mind. I hope you enjoyed the journey Nicholas and Cara had to make to grow and change.

Carolyne Aarsen

P.S. I love to hear from my readers. Drop me a note at carsen@xplornet.com or visit my Web site, www.carolyneaarsen.com to find out what's going on in my life and my writing.

QUESTIONS FOR DISCUSSION

1. What do you think is the main theme of this story?

2. How is that represented?

3. Which character could you identify the most with in this story and why?

4. Cara's mother seemed to think that it was more important to help needy children in other countries than her own child. What are you thoughts on this?

5. Was Cara's mother right in her actions? Why or why not?

6. Money seems to be an issue for Nicholas. Why do you think that was?

7. Was he right in thinking this? Can you sympathize?

8. What was your reaction to Cara's initial ultimatum to Nicholas? Was she right in her expectations?

9. In what way does the story show Cara's change in her attitude? Is there a change?

10. Who do you think had to make the biggest change in his or her attitude in this story and how was that portrayed?

11. In my stories I often deal with the repercussions on children of decisions made by parents. Have you had to look at your own life and deal with things your parents have done to you? What were the results?

12. Have you ever had to look at your own life and wonder about the repercussions of some of your decisions on your children's lives? And if not your children, then brothers? Sisters? Cousins?

13. Was the ending of this book realistic? Why or why not?

14. What did you learn from this story?

LARGER-PRINT BOOKS!

GET 2 FREE
LARGER-PRINT NOVELS
PLUS 2 FREE
MYSTERY GIFTS

Larger-print novels are now available...

YES! Please send me 2 FREE LARGER-PRINT Love Inspired® novels and my 2 FREE mystery gifts (gifts are worth about $10). After receiving them, if I don't wish to receive any more books, I can return the shipping statement marked "cancel". If I don't cancel, I will receive 6 brand-new novels every month and be billed just $4.74 per book in the U.S. or $5.24 per book in Canada. That's a saving of over 20% off the cover price. It's quite a bargain! Shipping and handling is just 50¢ per book.* I understand that accepting the 2 free books and gifts places me under no obligation to buy anything. I can always return a shipment and cancel at any time. Even if I never buy another book, the two free books and gifts are mine to keep forever.

122/322 IDN E7QP

Name	(PLEASE PRINT)

Address		Apt. #

City	State/Prov.	Zip/Postal Code

Signature (if under 18, a parent or guardian must sign)

Mail to **Steeple Hill Reader Service:**
IN U.S.A.: P.O. Box 1867, Buffalo, NY 14240-1867
IN CANADA: P.O. Box 609, Fort Erie, Ontario L2A 5X3

Not valid to current subscribers to Love Inspired Larger-Print books.

Are you a current subscriber to Love Inspired books and want to receive the larger-print edition?
Call 1-800-873-8635 or visit www.morefreebooks.com.

* Terms and prices subject to change without notice. Prices do not include applicable taxes. Sales tax applicable in N.Y. Canadian residents will be charged applicable provincial taxes and GST. Offer not valid in Quebec. This offer is limited to one order per household. All orders subject to approval. Credit or debit balances in a customer's account(s) may be offset by any other outstanding balance owed by or to the customer. Please allow 4 to 6 weeks for delivery. Offer available while quantities last.

Your Privacy: Steeple Hill Books is committed to protecting your privacy. Our Privacy Policy is available online at www.SteepleHill.com or upon request from the Reader Service. From time to time we make our lists of customers available to reputable third parties who may have a product or service of interest to you. If you would prefer we not share your name and address, please check here. ☐

Help us get it right—We strive for accurate, respectful and relevant communications. To clarify or modify your communication preferences, visit us at www.ReaderService.com/consumerschoice.

Love Inspired®
SUSPENSE
RIVETING INSPIRATIONAL ROMANCE

Watch for our new series of
edge-of-your-seat suspense novels.
These contemporary tales
of intrigue and romance
feature Christian characters
facing challenges to their faith...
and their lives!

NOW AVAILABLE IN REGULAR & LARGER-PRINT FORMATS

Steeple Hill®

Visit:
www.SteepleHill.com